"I don't know how we ever ended up together in the first place."

She regretted the words the moment they left her lips. When would she learn not to wave the red flag in front of the bull just because she was angry?

Jack's eyes lit alarmingly and traced a path down her body, leaving her skin tingling again in their wake. A slow half smile crossed his face. "Oh, I think you remember why, Bren," he said quietly. "I know I do."

She was close enough to feel the heat radiating off his body. A rush of desire slammed into her, making her knees wobble and her heart beat faster. He traced a finger over her collarbone and down the top of her arm. A shiver moved through her.

"We've always had this...."

Sex wouldn't solve anything. *It never had,* she reminded herself. They'd been down this path many, many times. Fight bitterly, then have fabulous make-up sex. It never made anything better.

She *had* to remember that. No matter how much her body begged to differ. No matter how strong the ache was.

No matter how much she wanted him.

KIMBERLY LANG hid romance novels behind her textbooks in junior high, and even a master's program in English couldn't break her obsession with dashing heroes and happily ever after. A ballet dancer turned English teacher, Kimberly married an electrical engineer and turned her life into an ongoing episode of *When Dilbert Met Frasier.* She and her Darling Geek live in beautiful north Alabama with their Amazing Child—who, unfortunately, shows an aptitude for sports.

Visit Kimberly at www.booksbykimberly.com for the latest news—and don't forget to say hi while you're there!

BOARDROOM RIVALS, BEDROOM FIREWORKS!

KIMBERLY LANG

~ Back in His Bed ~

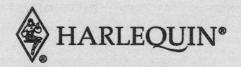

HARLEQUIN®

TORONTO • NEW YORK • LONDON
AMSTERDAM • PARIS • SYDNEY • HAMBURG
STOCKHOLM • ATHENS • TOKYO • MILAN • MADRID
PRAGUE • WARSAW • BUDAPEST • AUCKLAND

ISBN-13: 978-0-373-52787-8

BOARDROOM RIVALS, BEDROOM FIREWORKS!

First North American Publication 2010.

Copyright © 2010 by Kimberly Lang.

BOARDROOM RIVALS, BEDROOM FIREWORKS!

This one is for my mom.

If books are like children, then this book was me at fifteen: headstrong, occasionally willful and not afraid to do its own thing. But based on your example, I just kept faith in it, and it turned out to be fabulous and totally worth it in the end (hopefully also like me!). I love you, Mom. Thanks for putting up with me.

CHAPTER ONE

"THEY'RE ready, Brenna. I'll call Marco and tell him to have the crews here in the morning."

"It's too soon." Brenna double-checked the number on the refractometer in shock. No one else in Sonoma had grapes ripe this early; that was for sure. "We should have a couple of more weeks, at least."

"You doubt me?" Ted's affront was only partially feigned, and, though they'd been friends and coworkers for years, Brenna rushed to smooth the ruffled feathers of her viticulturist.

"Not at all. No one knows these vines better than you. I'm surprised, that's all."

Placated, Ted popped a grape into his mouth and chewed, a small, blissful smile crossing his face. "Obviously these grapes like our sunny summers and this drought. You just don't want to harvest in the heat."

"True." But that was only part of it. The new tanks had only arrived last week and were stacked haphazardly around the building. The main pump was still being temperamental, and there was so much paperwork left to do...and...and...she *needed* those couple of extra weeks just to finish getting her head together. She wasn't ready to start the crush right now.

Brenna looked at the vines, all heavy with ripe fruit—fruit that wasn't going to hold on while she adjusted to the new situation at a leisurely pace. Amante Verano Cellars was her responsibility now.

Well, mostly.

Ready or not, these grapes were coming in. She knew what to do; she'd been doing it her entire life. But she'd never done it alone. That responsibility weighed heavily on her shoulders.

"I just wish Max were here." The sigh in Ted's voice brought her back to reality with a jerk.

"I know. These vines were Max's ticket to wine-world domination—or at the very least a gold medal." She smiled weakly at Ted as her inspection of the grapes digressed to aimless fiddling. "He really should be here for this. It's not fair." She blinked back the tears threatening to escape again. She couldn't fall apart in front of Ted—or anyone else. Max would expect her to solider on, and everyone at Amante Verano needed to believe she had this under control. "Call Marco. We'll have the first grapes in the tank by tomorrow night."

They walked up the hill together, stopping occasionally to test the sugars and make notes on the grapes on different acres. The other vines were being slightly more predictable in their timelines. Another two weeks—give or take—and they'd be ready. September would be high-gear time.

"Have you talked to Jack yet?" Ted asked the question too quietly, too casually.

Her heart thumped in her chest at the mention of his name. "Not since the funeral, and then only for a minute." And that had been awkward and difficult, not to mention painful on more levels than she cared to admit. She'd exchanged condolences, shaken his hand and left. End of story.

"Does he know?"

"Oh, I'm sure he does. Max's lawyer called me to explain the partnership and what it meant, and I have to assume Jack was the first to know."

"And?" Ted was the first to brave asking the question she knew was on everyone's mind.

"There is no 'and.' I'm sure Jack has his hands full with the hotels, and the lawsuit against the driver that hit Max's car, and everything else, so we've got to be pretty low on the priority list." Max's death had left them all scrambling these last few weeks, just trying to sort out the wide range of Max's businesses and projects. In a way it had helped her grieve as well; she hadn't been able to lose herself in her grief as she'd wanted to, and the pain seemed a little easier to deal with when she could concentrate on keeping Max's beloved winery running smoothly.

Ted didn't look relieved.

"After the crush I'll make an appointment with the lawyers and we'll get it all sorted out." She patted his shoulder fondly. "Go on home. We've got several very busy days ahead of us."

"In other words, I should see my daughter while I can?"

"Yep." The crush would give them all something to

focus on. And when it was over she would have proved to everyone she was more than capable of shouldering the responsibility Max left her.

"Do you want to come to the house for dinner? You know you're always welcome, and Dianne will happily feed you."

It was tempting, very tempting, but she really needed to learn to cope on her own. Dianne had been mothering her way too much in the weeks since Max had died, and she needed to be strong now. She needed to be a grown-up. "Thanks, but no. Give my goddaughter a kiss for me, though, okay?"

"Will do." With a wave, Ted was gone, leaving her standing in the shadow of the main house alone, while his long legs covered the distance to the little house quickly. She could see the lights on upstairs in the apartment over the wine shop, which he shared with Dianne and baby Chloe.

She'd left a light on in the house as well, because she hadn't gotten used to coming home to a silent and dark house yet. She wondered if she ever would. Maybe after the craziness of the crush was over she'd get a puppy. It would keep her company, make the house feel less empty, and give her someone to talk to when she got home at night.

Her footsteps echoed in the hallway as habit directed her toward the office—just *her* office now, since Max was gone—where the winery's paperwork waited for her. As always, the work gave her something to do, a way to fill the long evenings.

Pressing "play" on the stereo filled the room with

music and chased the dreadful silence away. Max's huge desk dominated the space, and she turned her chair away from his empty one as she tried to focus on the invoices and orders that kept her inbox overflowing no matter how much time she spent on them.

But her usual focus wouldn't come. Ted's earlier question had brought everything she was trying so hard to repress right back to the forefront of her mind.

Amante Verano would make it to the top of Jack's to-do list eventually, and she had no idea how she'd handle that once it did. Avoidance—her time-honored and safe way of dealing with anything Jack-related—wasn't going to work this time. She had to make this work, because she couldn't run a business if she couldn't talk to her business partner.

The thought of Jack brought up all kinds of feelings she didn't want to deal with. Their history was just too complicated to pretend it didn't exist. Max had been her mentor, her friend, her surrogate father, and she, Max, and her mom had been a happy—if slightly oddly configured—family. Jack, not solely by his choice, had never been a part of that. Add in their private history, and the whole mess would put any soap opera plot to shame.

But she'd have to meet with Jack eventually. The thought kicked her heartbeat up a notch, and all the cleansing breaths in the world couldn't help calm it. She needed to be an adult about this. She needed to concentrate on the present and not let the past interfere.

Her glib response to Ted was starting to sound pretty good: a meeting on neutral ground, with lawyers doing most of the talking so she wouldn't have to. This was business, not personal, and surely she could swallow all the competing emotions long enough to get through a business meeting.

Many years ago Jack had told her how important it was to keep her personal life from rolling over into her business dealings. "Don't ever let one affect the other," he'd said. It was a major point of pride with him, and it seemed to work well as he expanded Garrett Properties all down the west coast.

Jack would want to keep this strictly business. If she could do that, it would make things a lot easier. For everyone, but most especially for her and her sanity.

Brenna took a deep breath, feeling a little better after her self-therapy session. They could come to a workable situation. One that was business only and ignored all the messiness of the past.

The fact she'd been crazy enough to marry him once wouldn't be a problem at all.

Jack sincerely hoped insanity didn't run in the family. That Max's will was merely an act of early-onset senility caused by too much wine over the years, or even some kind of weird joke on Max's part. There had to be an explanation, and he'd love to have just five minutes with his father to find out what the punch line was supposed to be.

Otherwise, insanity was the only explanation he had for the fact he now owned half of a winery in Sonoma. Him *personally*—not the company.

And the other half belonged to Brenna Walsh.

Brenna should be a footnote in his dating history—a cautionary tale about youthful infatuation and reckless decision-making—not a recurring character in his life.

Bad decisions must go hand-in-hand with anything Brenna-related, because he spent most of the drive out to Sonoma questioning his decision to handle this in person. His attorney, Roger, had offered to take care of it, but for some unknown reason, he felt this was a discussion he and Brenna should have face-to-face. The closer he got to the vineyard and Brenna, though, the more he realized this probably wasn't the best idea he'd ever had. God knew he had enough work on his desk waiting for him, and his trip to New York to negotiate the expansion of Garrett Properties should be his main focus right now, but he'd decided to get this off his plate first.

He rolled his eyes. He should have waited, gotten through more important, more pressing issues first, instead of letting his desire to cut ties with this place override his common sense.

The vines almost covering the sign welcoming him to Amante Verano had matured in the five years since he'd been out here for Brenna's mother's funeral, and grapes hung heavily from the canopy. As he turned on to the property the acres of vines laid out in perfectly aligned rows, the white stucco house at the top of the hill, and the weathered wooden winery building created a picturesque scene straight out of a movie's stock footage file.

Change came slowly to Amante Verano—if it ever

came at all—and it looked much the same as it had when Max had bought the winery twelve years ago.

That had been before Max's hobby had turned into his obsession. Before he'd left San Francisco for good and moved out here full-time to play in his grapes. Before Jack had become the Garrett in charge of Garrett Properties and the responsibility had consumed his entire life.

He drove slowly past the little house—that was Brenna's free and clear now, even if Max *had* converted it into the winery's shop once Brenna and her mother had moved into the main house—and noted the gravel parking lot was empty. Well, it was still early in the day for the tourists on their trips to wine country.

Where to find Brenna? Her lab? The office? He just wanted this over and done with as quickly as possible, so he could get back to civilization and his life. This place hung like an albatross around his neck, and the sooner he could get Brenna's signature on the documents, the better.

He didn't even *like* wine, for God's sake.

As he crested the next low hill he could see a tractor lumbering its way in the direction of the winery, the trailer overflowing with grapes.

He had never learned the intricacies of grape-growing or wine-making, and what little he had picked up he'd tried hard to forget, but even he knew it was early for harvesting. A strange turn of events, but it answered his first question nicely.

Brenna would be somewhere in those damn vines.

He sighed. He could either trudge through the

vineyard looking for her, or he could wait at the house until she was finished for the day.

"Let's just get this over with," he muttered to himself.

Cursing the entire ridiculous situation, Jack took his overnight case and laptop into the house, dropped them in what had used to be his room, and headed down the hill on foot to find his ex-wife.

"Brenna, they need you at the building. The pump's acting up again," Ted called from the end of the row she was working on. "Rick kicked it and nothing happened, so he asked me to get you."

Brenna sighed. The new pump was on backorder, and wouldn't be here until sometime in the next couple of weeks. Which would have been in plenty of time for the crush if Ted's grapes had kept to their usual timetable. "Did he kick it in the right place?"

Ted nodded. "Twice."

Straightening, she slid her clippers into her back pocket and pulled off her gloves, before wiping a hand across her sweaty forehead. "Great. Exactly what I didn't want to do today. Do you have this under control?"

"Of course. I didn't need you out here to begin with," he teased.

They didn't have time for this, and they would only get further behind if she had to take the whole pump apart again. Beads of sweat rolled down her spine, and she grimaced at the feeling. At least she'd be out of the heat sooner than planned. She'd call Dianne and get her to bring a clean shirt along with their lunches.

She pulled her cellphone out of her other pocket, replacing it with her gloves. Dialing Dianne as she walked, she didn't see the man who stepped into her path until she ran face-first into him. The force knocked her hat off her head, and the cellphone hit the dust at her feet.

"Sorry," she said, as strong hands closed around her arms to steady her. In the split second that followed her brain registered the fine cotton shirt—far too nice for any of her guys to be wearing while they worked—the strangely familiar feeling of the man's grasp, and the subtle spicy scent tickling her nostrils.

And then her brain shut down altogether as one thought crystallized: *Jack.*

"It's a bit early to be harvesting, isn't it, Brenna?"

His deep voice rumbled through her, causing her brain to misfire in shock, but the bite of sarcasm brought her world back into focus. Shrugging off his hands in what she hoped was a casual way, she tried to match his tone. "The grapes are ready when the grapes are ready. You should know that."

She made the mistake of meeting his eyes when she spoke, and the smoky blue stare caused her to take a step back. She bent to retrieve her hat, but as she stood, she saw the assessing roaming those eyes made down her body, taking in her sweat-darkened T-shirt, battered jeans, and dusty work boots before settling back on her face.

She just hoped the flush she felt on her cheeks looked like a response to the heat of the sun, not the heat of his stare.

One of his dark eyebrows arched up at her in surprise

as she captured her ponytail under her hat and pulled the brim down to shade her eyes.

"You really need a new hat, Brenna. That one's seen better days."

Damn it, he'd recognized it. Jack had bought her this hat—a silly gift from the early days of their relationship—and if she'd had even the smallest clue he'd show up she'd have left it at the house today. It was her favorite hat—wide brimmed and very comfortable— and she'd absolutely only kept it because it worked so well for her, *not* because it was a gift from him.

She hoped he didn't think otherwise.

Brazening it out regardless, she lifted her chin. "It's perfectly serviceable." Shifting her weight onto her heels, she put her hands in her back pockets and tried to act normally, although she felt anything but normal. Her heart pounded in her chest and her palms felt clammy. *Be an adult.* "What brings you to Amante Verano, Jack?"

Her words seemed to amuse him. "I know the lawyer explained Max's will to you. You had to be expecting me."

"Actually, no. I was expecting another phone call from your *lawyer*—not a personal visit from you." This was the longest conversation they'd had in over five years, and she wasn't handling it well. She knew she sounded defensive and prickly.

"We don't need lawyers for this." He pulled a folded manila envelope from the back pocket of his jeans. "If we could go somewhere quiet—"

Somewhere quiet. Brenna's knees wobbled a little bit

at the rush of memories those two words brought. That summer after graduation, when finding "somewhere quiet" had always led to…

She shook herself, forcing the memories and the tingle they caused back into the past, where they belonged. Concentrating on the envelope in his hand helped; she had a very sick feeling she wasn't going to like what was in there, otherwise Jack wouldn't have wanted to take the conversation elsewhere. Hoping for steadiness in her voice—if not her knees—she met his eyes. "In case you haven't noticed, I'm a little busy at the moment. Surely you remember how this place works?"

"Brenna…" The muscle in Jack's jaw tightened, showing his frustration with her.

That helped. Irritation flowed through her body, displacing the earlier, more disturbing emotions. Jack was *not* going to walk onto her property after all these years and act as if he owned the damn place. Okay, so he owned half of it, and the guilt that she was the reason he never came out here anymore nagged at her a bit, but still… She focused on her irritation.

He wasn't the boss of Amante Verano. Or her. Whatever was so all-fire important enough to pull him away from the excitement of his life in the city could just wait. "I have grapes losing quality while I stand here talking to you, and I need to go fix a stupid pump if I want to get them into the tanks tonight. You'll just have to wait your turn."

Pleased with herself for getting the last word, she brushed past him, intent on getting to the winery and back to work. Jack grabbed her arm, halting her steps and pulling her too close for comfort. His face was only inches from hers—something her body reacted to instantly. And embarrassingly.

Heat, *real* heat, the kind she hadn't felt in years, surged through her. He was so close she could see herself in the pupils of his eyes, smell the spicy scent of his soap. She swallowed hard. "Not now, Jack. I'm—"

"Busy, I know. So am I. Do you think I *wanted* to come out here?" His dark brows pulled together in a sharp vee as he gritted out the words.

He might as well have slapped her. The pain and shock were the same. In a way, she welcomed it. It would help her focus on the present.

Then the heat dropped out of his voice. "I'm selling my half of the winery."

Outrage replaced her shock. *What?* "You can't. Max set up the partnership—"

"Oh, I'm well aware of how this ridiculous partnership is set up. It's barely legal and completely beyond reason. But I've found a buyer, and all you have do is sign off on it."

She hadn't planned on owning Amante Verano right now either—much less sharing it with him—but he didn't have the right to go selling off his part of it. His attitude wasn't exactly helping the situation any either. "There's no way in hell I'm signing anything. I'm sorry if you find the arrangement distasteful. Trust me, it's not exactly a picnic for me either. But we're stuck with each other."

"You won't have to be stuck with me once you sign off on the sale."

The grip on her arm was bordering on painful, and

she smacked his hand away. He stepped back, the muscle in his jaw still working.

She bristled. "To whom? Let me guess: you found someone who fancied the odd break from city life and wanted to come stomp grapes on the weekends?" The look on Jack's face told her all she needed to know. "That figures. My answer is no."

"That's not an option, Brenna. I don't want a winery. Not even half of one."

Bless Max for his forward-thinking and iron-clad partnership clauses. Otherwise she'd be royally screwed about now. "Tough. I'm certainly not turning half of everything Max and I worked for over to someone who doesn't know squat about this business."

"You'd rather deal with me? Isn't that worse?"

How could she explain her reasoning to Jack? It barely made sense to her. And would it make any difference if she did? "I'll take the devil I know any day."

Jack opened his mouth to argue, but her phone rang. A quick glance at the number reminded her of all the things she needed to be doing instead of standing here fighting with Jack. "I'm going to go take a pump apart now, because I have wine to make. This conversation is over."

This time Jack didn't move to stop her—which was a good thing, because with her temper riding so high she would probably take a swing at him if he tried. But it didn't stop him from flinging the last word at her back as she stalked off.

"This is not over, Brenna. Put *that* in your damn tank and ferment it."

* * *

Jack let her stomp away, recognizing the signs of a full-on Brenna fit brewing even after ten years. She had her shoulders thrown back and her head high, but he could tell she was talking to herself by the agitated movements of her hands.

Maybe confronting Brenna like that had been a slight tactical error. He'd let his desire to get this over with override his business sense. Hell, his common sense seemed to have checked out—as it always did with Brenna.

It was the only explanation he had.

He'd had the whole conversation planned—he knew Brenna well enough to know how to approach her—but when she'd slammed into him his body had remembered each and every curve of her and promptly forgotten his earlier plan. Then his hands had curved around her biceps, and the muscles there had flexed in response…and he'd felt the tiny shudder move through her when she'd realized who he was.

He should have known Brenna would react like this to his news. It wasn't as if their history didn't complicate this situation even more than it should have been. When you added in Brenna's temper… What was it Max had said shortly after Brenna and her equally copper-headed mother had moved in? "The only things I've learned to fear are red-headed women and downhill putts." Since Jack didn't play golf—he simply didn't have the time or patience for the game—he'd dismissed both warnings at the time. He'd learned the hard way the truth of at least half of

Max's statement. Pity he'd forgotten it before he came out here.

He should have let his lawyer handle this instead of thinking he and Brenna could do it the easy way. Hell, hadn't he learned long ago that nothing with Brenna was easy?

With a sigh of disgust, he folded the envelope again and put it back in his pocket. Tonight, after Brenna had the day's harvest safely in the tanks, they'd talk again.

She couldn't put him off forever, and the house, while large, wasn't big enough for her to avoid him. Red hair aside, Brenna's anger rarely had lasting power, so that would work in his favor as well.

He still had to go through some files in Max's office, but even with the delay caused by Brenna he should have plenty of time to deal with her, take care of business, and get the hell out of Sonoma tomorrow.

CHAPTER TWO

SHOWER. Dinner. Drink. The thought of those three rewards kept Brenna's legs moving as she dragged herself back to the house, but the black Mercedes parked next to her Jeep was an unwelcome reminder of Jack's presence. Not that she needed one. He'd been circling her thoughts all afternoon, distracting her and keeping her temper on edge. While she'd bemoaned rattling around the house alone recently, Jack wasn't exactly the company she'd been hoping for.

She left her boots in the mudroom and headed straight for the safety of her bedroom. Jack must be holed up in his old room, because the house still echoed like it always did these days. Technically, Jack's room was the guest suite now, but Max had always held out hope that Jack would make use of it again one day.

And now he was. It had only taken Max's death and inheriting half the winery to get him back out here. That familiar guilt settled on her again as the shower washed away the dirt from the vineyard and she scrubbed the grease from the pump from under her fingernails. Max had never said anything to her face, but Brenna knew that deep down he had to blame her, to *resent* her for Jack's absence and the breach in his relationship with his son.

She'd been trying to make that up to Max every day for the last ten years, at the very least by making his winery everything Max had wanted it to be. Even if he'd made it more difficult for her now, by bringing Jack into the mix. Rationally, she knew why Max had split the vineyard between them, but it was still a difficult situation to handle.

The confrontation in the vineyard with Jack still had her cringing. Could she have been more juvenile and defensive? In all of the possible scenarios she'd imagined, Jack accosting her in her vineyard with some crazy idea about selling to a stranger had never crossed her mind. Not to mention how totally unprepared she'd been to actually be that close to him again. It had taken her an hour just to calm down.

She turned off the water and sighed. If this wasn't a disaster, she didn't want to know what was. Amante Verano had always been the one stable pillar in her life, her haven, and now even that foundation was shaking. She needed some time to think. And food.

Her stomach was growling loudly by the time she'd dried off and slid into a clean pair of pajamas, so she left her hair to dry naturally and padded to the kitchen in search of something to eat.

Dianne, bless her, had left a plate in the fridge for her, and in less time than it took for her to pour a glass of wine her dinner was ready. She took her plate to the counter and grabbed the TV remote.

Just as she took the first bite Jack walked in, causing her to choke on Dianne's homemade quiche.

A black sleeveless T-shirt exposed shoulder and arm muscles covered in a sheen of sweat. Gym shorts rode low on his hips, giving her a glimpse of tight abs between the hem of the shirt and the waistband as he reached into the cupboard for a glass and then filled it with water. Powerful thighs. Defined calves.

Mercy.

Oh, she remembered his body all too well—and far too frequently—but to have it displayed for her in reality had her coughing painfully as her mouth went dry and it became hard to chew. A look of concern crossed Jack's face and he reached for her.

She did not need him touching her. Even if it was for the Heimlich maneuver. Waving him away, she swallowed with difficulty.

Jack offered her his water, and she waved that away as well; the thought of sharing his glass just seemed too familiar and intimate. She reached for her own glass, but the normally smooth wine burned her throat on the way down. She coughed one last time and willed herself under control.

It didn't quite work, but at least she wasn't choking now. She forced her eyes back to his face. "I see you found Max's gym."

"I did. Nice set-up you've got in there." Jack's eyebrows went up as he belatedly noted her pajamas, and Brenna felt a flush rise on her neck. *Get real. They're just pajamas. Boring ones at that. Just eat.*

"Max seemed to think we needed one, but I never

have understood why." *Stab, lift, bite, chew, swallow.* "We tend to get our exercise the old-fashioned way around here."

Don't stare, for God's sake.

"I remember."

Jack leaned against the other side of the counter, and she could feel those blue eyes boring into her. She concentrated on eating, ignoring the impulse to take her plate to her room. The weight of his stare, though, got to be too much. "*Must* you watch me eat?"

"You're a bit hostile tonight." Calmly enough to make her even more jumpy, Jack lifted his glass and drank.

Mirroring his calm, she placed her fork carefully on her plate. "You expected something different?" She latched on to the easiest excuse, the one that was much easier to deal with. "You come storming out here, telling me you want to sell out—without any discussion at all—and I'm supposed to be happy about it? Get real, Jack."

A bead of sweat trickled down the side of his face and he swiped at it, giving her another quick glimpse of his abs as his shirt rose. A familiar heat settled low in her belly. "You want reality? Good. We can skip past all the small talk and get straight down to business."

His tone doused the heat nicely. Brenna straightened her spine and tried to pretend she was wearing more than a pair of thin cotton pajamas. "Business. Excellent. As you saw, we have an early set of grapes coming in—a hybrid vine Max and Ted have been babying along for the last couple of years. I'm going to make an excellent, yet deceptively simple white from them, and it's going to put Amante Verano on the map." She stood and moved around the counter, put her plate into the dishwasher. "I'll be sure to let you know when it's ready to taste."

Jack hadn't moved, and getting to the dishwasher had put her in close proximity to him. So close she caught his scent, reigniting that heat again. She tried to breathe shallowly through her mouth as she closed the machine and stood to face him.

"Brenna, don't."

Feigning innocence, she met his eyes. "Don't what? Talk business?"

He crossed his arms across his chest casually, looking completely unruffled—to someone who didn't know him, at least. She, however, knew better, and his next words confirmed it. "I could not care less what you're doing with those grapes—or any of the grapes. I just want you to sign off on the sale."

"In case I was unclear earlier, I'll sign off when hell freezes over. You're not selling half of this place to some stranger."

In that same even tone—the one that meant he was only barely keeping his frustration with her in check— he asked, "Then what *do* you want, Brenna?"

"I want you to go back to San Francisco. Go run your empire and leave Amante Verano—" *and me*, she added silently "—alone." The words came out in a rush, and she took a deep breath to stem the flow. "You can be a silent partner—just let us do our thing, and we'll mail you a check for your share of the profits."

"Profits?" He laughed, a mean humorless sound that stabbed her. "This place is nothing but a money pit. Without Max's bankroll—"

"We had a couple of lean years, yes, but we're about to turn a corner. Do you have any idea how long it takes for a winery to become profitable? *Years*, Jack. We're nearly there, *ahead* of all our predictions."

"I've seen your books, Bren."

Bren. The nickname caught her off-guard, throwing her momentarily. "Then you know what I'm saying is true."

"It doesn't matter. How many times do I have to tell you that I don't want a winery?"

Her frustration was starting to build, and she wished she had the ability to control it like Jack. "It's just a winery, for God's sake, not a brothel."

He snorted. "No, brothels are profitable."

"And so are wineries. You just have to be patient. Not that you'd have any idea what *that* concept is like," she added under her breath.

"Brenna…" Impatience tinged his voice, and the muscle in his jaw was working again.

Enough defense. Time to take offense. "Who's being hostile now?"

"If I'm hostile, it's only because you're being completely unreasonable. Again."

Talk about a time warp. Less than a day and they were already settling back into their fighting stances. Oh, she'd love to throw something at him. "Don't start."

His fingers tightened around his biceps. "I'd love to finish, actually."

She took a step back. "Why are you so hot to sell? This is Max's legacy."

"Max's legacy is Garrett Properties."

There was that sting of the slap again. "So would you be so quick to sell off a piece of that?"

"If the price were right and the situation called for it, yes. It's called business, Brenna." He finally levered himself out of his casual lounging against the counter, and suddenly she felt as if she should keep something between them. This would be easier with a barrier keeping him from looming over her.

"There's the difference, Jack. This is more than just a business for me. It's more than a paycheck and a profit margin. It's my *home*. It's all I've ever wanted and you know that."

"Really, Bren? *This* is what you want?"

The question shook her, but she fought not to let it show. Instead, she crossed her arms, copying his earlier casual stance. "Of course."

Jack looked at her strangely, and she struggled to keep her face impassive. "Since when?"

Another memory slammed into her. *Of course* Jack would have to remember the *one* thing she'd hoped he would forget. "It's been a while, Jack. People change."

That damn eyebrow quirked up again. "Obviously."

Don't let this turn personal. Focus on the business. "I'll buy you out."

Jack looked at her in surprise. "You have that kind of money squirreled away someplace? I'm impressed, Bren."

"Well, no." She paced as she tried to think fast. "I can't do it now, but I will eventually. Maybe a little at a time over the next few years…"

"I'm not shackling myself to this place indefinitely."

That's right. He was just as trapped as she was with this partnership. That knowledge gave her a little spurt of courage and she smiled. "Then we seem to be at a stalemate." Oh, that *had* to bother him, and the narrowing of his eyes told her she was right. She could end the night on a high note. "I'm going to bed. I have to get up early to get the grapes in. Make yourself at home. Or, better yet, go home. We're done here."

He stepped in front of her, blocking her path of retreat. Once again she was too close to his body, and her libido reacted immediately. "No, we're not."

She needed distance to get her body back under control, needed quiet and space to figure out what she was going to do. "Move."

"What? So you can stomp off again? Try to stall some more? Stave off the inevitable?"

She had to tilt her head back, but she met his hard stare. "Inevitable? Selling is inevitable? Hardly."

"If you knew a thing about business, you'd know there's no way this partnership can work as long as we're at odds. You can sell now, or lose everything later."

Cold prickles climbed her spine. "You wouldn't. You'd never intentionally let a business—*any* business— fail. It's not in your DNA."

Jack stepped back, finally giving her the space she needed, and she inhaled in relief. The relief quickly faded, though, as he tossed down the gauntlet. "There's a first time for everything, Brenna."

The sobering knowledge of what he was threatening settled around her. Granted, he couldn't sell without her approval, but he could certainly make it next to impossible for her to do business at all. That scenario had never occurred to her, but something in his eyes told her he could do it. *Would* do it. Easily. Her eyes burned at the thought, and she bit the inside of her mouth to distract herself with physical pain. She would *not* cry in front of him, not now. She couldn't get her voice above a whisper, though, when she asked, "Do you hate me that much?"

His eyes raked over her before he answered. "It's just business."

Oh, no, this crossed a line, no matter what he tried to say.

"Go ahead and stomp off now, Bren, but think about what I've said. We'll talk again tomorrow."

Her knees were trembling, but Brenna tried hard to keep her head up as she left the kitchen. Once in the safety of her bedroom, she closed the door and leaned against it before her legs could give out completely.

She'd never seen Jack like that. Not even after their last fight, when she'd packed her bags while Jack had called a car to bring her back here. When pushed, Jack turned silent and broody, not coldly calculating. And since Jack never made empty threats… Damn it. She'd been fooling herself to think they could move beyond their past and forge any kind of business relationship. She'd had no idea his dislike of her was so strong that he'd rather destroy everything Max had created out here than work with her.

She looked skyward. "Why'd you do this to me, Max?"

No answer came, and she flopped on the bed, wrung out, yet still jumpy from the evening.

Jack's sarcastic rebuttal of the one argument he really shouldn't be able to question had thrown her off her game. Of all the things for Jack to bring up... Hell, she'd practically forgotten; why hadn't he? Oh, the optimism and arrogance of an eighteen-year-old girl in love. She groaned and pulled the pillow over her head. Back then she'd figured Max and her mom would run Amante Verano forever. She, on the other hand, would take her knowledge out into the wide world, educating the masses on wine-making, visiting wineries in France and Italy and bringing new ideas back to their vineyard—in general, just getting the hell out of Sonoma and doing something more. Jack had embraced that idea, encouraged it.

But the wide world hadn't had a place for her, and she'd come home. Then her mom had died...

Amante Verano was where she belonged, it seemed. And she'd accepted that, thrown herself into it, made it her life.

She couldn't let Jack undermine that. Not now. No matter how much Jack hated it.

Or her.

For the second time that day Jack let Brenna stomp away, wondering when he'd lost his lauded ability to finesse a situation. What had possessed him to think he'd be able to handle this negotiation just like any other of the hundreds he'd done? Make the plan, work the plan—common sense and good business tactics had always worked for him before. Except when it came to Brenna. Bren just knew the right buttons to push to cause him to lose his temper—a hard pill to swallow, since he never let his temper loose any other time.

Hell, who was he kidding? Brenna *was* his button. Nothing between them had ever been steady or calm or predictable. It was all drama and tension and theatrics.

Oh, they'd started with a bang. But once the initial glow had faded their relationship had fallen apart with alarming speed. All the dreams and plans and excitement had crumbled under the strain of reality, and "love" just hadn't been enough. Before long they'd just made each other miserable.

Except in bed. The familiar heat spread over his skin. Making love to Brenna was like holding a live fuse too close to the gunpowder: hot, dangerous, explosive.

And ultimately destructive.

But they'd been young then, too young and stupid to realize sex wasn't enough to hold them together until it was too late. No matter how great it was.

If tonight was any indication, his body hadn't forgotten *that* in the intervening years. Her plain, most-likely organic cotton pajamas did a good job of camouflaging what was underneath, but his body had reacted anyway, reigniting that old urge to get her under him as quickly as humanly possible.

But reality hit home pretty quickly once Brenna started in on him. While his hands had still itched to touch her, he'd been reminded exactly why they were in this mess in the first place.

Regardless of their past or their present, he didn't necessarily relish the idea of destroying her dreams for this place. But that didn't mean he wanted to be a part of it, either. Max might have found someone willing to build his little wine-making dynasty, but Jack didn't want to play along. And, Brenna, for all her talk of a partnership, couldn't really want him around either.

Not after everything.

He needed something stronger than water to drink. A look around revealed several bottles of wine but little else, and nothing of interest. Wine on the counters, wine in the cupboards, wine in the largest non-commercial fridge he'd ever seen. Was there a damn beer anywhere on the property?

Max would have Scotch in his desk. He always did. His passion for wine-making couldn't have squelched his love of a good single malt.

Jack had to pass Brenna's bedroom to get to the office. Light escaped around the doorframe, but the room was silent as he paused in front of the door, debating whether he'd made a mistake in letting Brenna walk out in the middle of their discussion.

Discussion? Right. He seemed incapable of having a civilized discussion with Brenna about anything. Between her temper and the emotional attachment she had to this place, the chances of any civil discourse seemed remote.

The Amante Verano business office was large—larger than such a small operation probably needed, but that was just Max's style—and Max's desk dominated the room. A smaller desk he assumed was Brenna's sat at an angle to Max's. He recognized the set-up; he'd learned the family business in much the same fashion—except the view from the offices of

Garrett Properties encompassed San Francisco Bay and the Golden Gate Bridge, not acres of vines.

The second drawer on the left-hand side produced the Scotch he had been looking for. He leaned back in Max's chair as he poured two fingers and contemplated Brenna's desk. His father had initially planned for that desk to be Jack's, from where he would run the winery as well as the hotels. It hadn't mattered that he didn't want to.

Hell, after Max had gotten over the shock of Jack and Brenna's elopement he'd been practically gleeful over the "merger." The divorce had given Jack a valid reason to stay away all these years, but it seemed Max was trying to have the final say after all.

"Sorry, old man. You can't make me run this place."

No matter what Brenna wanted to believe, she wasn't even the main reason he wanted out from under Amante Verano. Max's first business ate up enough of his life as it was, especially since Max had all but turned the hotels over to him completely once this winery had become his focus. The complication of Brenna didn't add any appeal, though.

His body disagreed, growing hard again at the thought of her. Good God, it had been ten years. Shouldn't he be past that by now?

He sipped the Scotch in silence for a few minutes, willing his body to get over it. When he heard a noise to his right, he looked up to see a barefoot Brenna slip quietly into the room.

"I thought you had to get up early in the morning."

Brenna jumped, a small cry escaping her as she

turned around to locate the voice. Her hand fell away from her throat as she found him, and her shoulders dropped. "Damn it, Jack, you scared the life out of me. What are you doing in here?"

He shrugged. "I could ask you the same thing."

"It's *my* office." Brenna's chin lifted in challenge.

Unable to resist prodding her, he raised the glass in salute. "And now it's half mine."

Brenna shook her head. "Whatever." She slid into her chair and turned her back to him as she booted up the computer. "I need to do some work, so if you'll excuse me…?"

She wanted him to retreat so she wouldn't have to? Hardly. "Go ahead. You won't bother me at all." Brenna's hands tightened around the armrests of her chair, and even in the semi-darkness of the room he could see the white knuckles. If he listened carefully, he'd probably be able to hear her grinding her teeth next.

He heard her sigh, then her fingers moved quickly across the keyboard, the clicking sound filling the silence. "The new hotel in Monterrey is selling the Pinot faster than I can get it to them. Max's idea to market our wines in your boutique hotels was a fabulous one."

"That's nice."

"It is." She pushed her hair over her shoulder, causing it to spill over the back of the chair, where the light bounced off it in a coppery glow. "It means you may be seeing those profit checks sooner than you thought."

That was supposed to convince him he wanted to own half a winery? "I don't need the money."

Brenna shrugged. "Good. I'll buy new tanks instead."

So much for polite conversation. "You just bought new tanks."

Brenna spun in her chair, sputtering. "Are you questioning—?"

He shouldn't prod her, but he just couldn't stop himself. "Yeah, I am. You just bought new tanks. Italian ones. Very expensive. I saw the invoice."

Bren straightened her spine, and she seemed to be trying for a lofty, all-business tone. "I'm slowly trying to replace all the old ones that desperately need it, and the best tanks come from Italy. Since the best equipment lets me make the best wines, it's money well spent." She took a deep breath. "Anyway, why are you poking around in my invoices? I thought you didn't care about this place."

"I don't. But since I now own half of it…" he loved the way her eyes narrowed every time he reminded her of that fact "…I have to make sure it's running properly. It's in my DNA, remember?"

"You know nothing about *this* business, so I think the silent partner idea is best."

"I don't do silent. Until I sell my half…" He let the sentence trail off and let her fill in the blanks.

It only took her a second to make the leap, and her hackles went up again. "Are you seriously planning to buck me on every decision I make around here?"

"Of course. Weren't you listening earlier?" Brenna's eyes widened, and he was lucky looks couldn't kill. "But you know it would be really easy to get me away from your books. Sign on the dotted line, Bren, and I'm out of your hair."

Brenna rolled her eyes and turned back to her computer. She started to type, then stopped as she leaned her head against the chair-back. "First you threaten to drive my winery into the ground. Then you threaten to drive me insane. To think Max used to say how good you'd be for this place."

"There's a simple solution, you know."

"It's not simple at all." She moved her chair slightly, turning her profile his way. Her eyes were closed, and her throat worked as she rubbed her hands over her face.

"It's a lot easier than you're making it, Bren. You don't want me in your business, and you know it. Sign off on the sale and I'm gone."

"I've already said no. Come up with a new idea."

Lord, the woman was stubborn. "There are no other ideas."

"You're going to tell me that the great Jack Garrett doesn't have a Plan B?"

He swirled the drink in his glass. "I don't need a Plan B."

Brenna turned to face him again, and her voice turned conciliatory for a change. "Max wanted Amante Verano kept as a small family business. He didn't want outsiders involved."

"And what, exactly, are *you*?"

Brenna pulled back as if she'd been hit, and he regretted the harshness of his words.

"That's unfair, Jack. We were a family, and this is a family business."

"Brenna—"

She held up a hand. "Wait. Just— Just—" She took another deep breath and faced him across the expanse of Max's desk. "I don't want to fight any more. Especially not with you."

"Then don't fight me. Neither of us wants to be in this situation."

She opened her mouth, then closed it and chewed on her bottom lip for a moment while she thought. "You're right, you know. I don't want you around anymore than you want to be here. But…" She took a deep breath. Her voice dropped to a whisper as she turned to meet his eyes. "I *need* you."

The desire that slammed into him with those three simple words nearly caused him to drop his glass. Oh, part of him knew she was still talking about the damn winery, but his body was reacting to that throaty whisper—she'd whispered those words in his ear countless times as she'd wrapped herself around him.

Need. She'd always referred to him as a need. He'd nearly forgotten, but the response of his body proved those six months they'd had weren't as deeply buried as he'd thought. He shifted in his chair, attempting to bring the reaction under control.

Brenna seemed not to notice. "Max was the brains behind the business. I'm sure you know that. And I could learn, but Amante Verano would suffer in the meantime. I know that's why Max put us in this partnership—he always said the Walsh women made great wine, but they needed Garrett men to make it profitable." She folded her hands in her lap, squeezing her fingers together as she talked. "It took me a while to figure out what he meant—beyond the MBA-approved business model, at least. The Garrett name opens a lot of doors."

"You should know that from experience. You were a Garrett for a short while."

She paled a bit at the reminder. "Don't go there, Jack. What I *mean* is that as long as there's a Garrett behind Amante Verano I can do business. Get loans to expand, for example. A small winery is a bank's nightmare—unless there's a Garrett on the books, of course, and then we're golden. I just need you to back me—in name, if not spirit—for a few years. That's all I'm asking."

"You ask a lot."

"Why? How? You don't have to do anything."

He just looked at her.

She nodded. "Except deal with me. And you hate that more than anything else."

He'd never heard Brenna sound so flat, so lifeless. He'd almost prefer her anger to that toneless resignation. "I don't hate you, Bren. But I'm not going to be your partner either."

She cocked her head. "Once bitten?" she challenged.

"I'm not afraid of your bite." In fact, the thought of her teeth on his skin brought back a slew of sensual memories. Unwilling to circle this topic again or battle with his body any longer, he stood. "Decide what you're going to do. I'll leave the sale paperwork in the kitchen."

Brenna's jaw dropped at his words, then she spun her chair back to her computer. He heard her mumble something under her breath as he turned to leave.

He doubted it was a compliment.

CHAPTER THREE

"I SWEAR, Di, it's frustrating. I just want to scream. Or something," she muttered. Brenna positioned her clippers and separated the grape cluster from the vine with a satisfying, overly forceful snip.

"Picturing Jack's neck, are we?" Dianne teased from the other side of the row of vines. Chloe napped peacefully in a carrier strapped to Dianne's chest, her hat with its embroidered Amante Verano logo shielding her fat baby cheeks from the early-morning sun.

"It's cathartic." She snipped two more clusters and added them to the bucket at her feet. "And safer for Jack."

"What are you going to do?" Dianne asked the question casually, but Brenna knew everyone in the vineyard was on edge, waiting to see what would happen next. Jack's plan to sell would affect everyone in some way.

"Honestly? I'm not sure. I'm open to ideas if you have any." She'd been up most of the night, tossing and turning as she tried to figure out her options. There weren't many.

"I wish I did."

"Stubborn. Arrogant. Domineering. Jerk." She punctuated each comment with a snip of the clippers.

"Max could be like that sometimes. He's his father's son; that's for sure."

Brenna laughed. "Oh, I dare you to tell him that. It'll really get his goat."

"I don't think antagonizing Jack further is really the best idea right now, do you?" Dianne was always so calm, so unflappable. So annoyingly right most of the time.

"I was trying to be nice last night. Trying to be reasonable. That didn't work out so well."

"Because you have a history with Jack."

"*Ancient* history," Brenna clarified.

"Still, it complicates things."

No kidding. She'd seen the papers in the kitchen this morning; she'd even glanced through them while she waited for her coffee to brew. Turn over fifty-percent of the vineyard to the highest bidder? She'd been tempted to feed Jack's stack of papers into the shredder and leave a bag of confetti hanging on his doorknob.

For the thousandth time, she wished she had the money to buy Jack's share. But while the banks would be happy to loan her barrels of money as long as Jack was a co-owner, no bank in the world would loan her the money to buy him *out*. It still wasn't an ideal solution—buying Jack out only solved one problem while causing a whole slew of others.

In the small hours of the morning, though, she had realized how much of their current problem was rooted in their heated, reckless past. She needed to recognize it and figure out good ways to move past it. Dianne wasn't the only one realizing that. "That knowledge— however truthful it may be—doesn't make the situation suck any less." It certainly didn't make her feel any better. She was drowning—in anger, frustration, guilt, worry, and a dozen other emotions she couldn't quite name. The painful knot in her stomach was bordering on debilitating.

Dianne nodded understandingly, then looked at her watch. "I hate to harvest and run, but I need to shower so I can get the shop open in time. Plus, I think Chloe is waking up." Dianne cooed at the baby as she stripped off her gloves.

"I appreciate the help. And the company, of course. Getting up at dawn goes above and beyond the call of duty."

"But it's fun—at least for the first couple of hours," she added, as Brenna raised an eyebrow at her in disbelief. "Do you think you'll finish today?"

"Marco brought a full crew, so if not today definitely tomorrow."

"Good. I'll see you at lunch. Tuna salad okay with you?"

"That's great. You're the best."

"I know," Dianne tossed over her shoulder as she left.

Brenna had enjoyed the company—having Di to talk to had been a nice distraction, one that she missed as she fell back into her rhythm and her mind started to wander.

There *had* to be a solution. She just needed to find it. If she'd only known Jack would carry such a grudge...

It wasn't *all* her fault, she thought as she carried the full bucket of grapes to the bin at the end of the row and emptied it. He was just as much to blame for their disastrous relationship and the fallout as she was. The early days had been fantastic—the type of thing romance novels were written about. The boss's handsome son, descending from the city to sweep the winemaker's daughter off her feet. Picnics in the vineyard; stolen kisses behind the barrels of Merlot. Making love under a canopy of Cabernet vines, then feeding the ripe grapes to each other in the afterglow.

It had been everything she'd ever dreamed of. Romantic and passionate and all-encompassing. Jack had made her feel like the center of his universe—beautiful and sexy and interesting. It had been too easy to fall in love.

But, while opposites attracting worked great in movies, the reality hadn't been dreamy at all.

While it had all gone to hell later, she did have fond memories of being eighteen and head-over-heels in love. Jack had been different then, too: more carefree, with a smile that melted her knees even in memory.

The old Jack would be more reasonable and much easier for her to deal with. The old Jack wouldn't want to sell her winery out from under her, or ruin everything she'd worked for simply out of spite. He'd changed so much in the last ten years. He'd become more reserved, harder and colder. Sometimes she wondered if he was really the same man.

She missed the old Jack. The one she fell in love with. The Jack who didn't hate her.

She shook off the reverie and the sinking feeling. She had to deal with *this* Jack. And quickly—for the good of Amante Verano and her own mental health.

"Daydreaming on the job, boss?" Ted grinned at her as he upended his overflowing bucket into the bin. "You seem pretty far away."

"Trust me, I'm here. Just sending up quick prayers that the pump doesn't die again."

"After the way you cursed at it yesterday? It wouldn't dare."

She laughed. "It deserved it. Cantankerous thing." *Much like someone else she knew.* She pulled off her gloves. "Unless you need me here for some reason, I'm going to head back to the winery. Lots of grapes to process, and…"

"You have a cantankerous pump to deal with," he finished for her.

That explanation would do. "Exactly."

But the pump seemed to be working fine. At least that part of her life was moving along on plan. Although it freed her mind to stew over other issues for the next six hours, she didn't discover any new solutions to her problems.

She took her time hosing out the crusher for the last time, then puttered around the lab, stalling for time. Calling it a day would put her back in the house with Jack. For such a big house, it felt very small with Jack in it, and, since she was still having trouble controlling her hormones while he was around, putting herself in close proximity to him didn't sound like a great idea. Plus, there was no way to avoid more discussion of the future of the vineyard, and without any bright new ideas she wasn't in any hurry for another round with Jack over *that*.

But she couldn't hide in her lab forever, and as the

sun went down her irritation grew—both with herself and Jack. She was avoiding her *home*, for goodness's sake. Just because of *him*.

That irritation fueled her up the hill to the house, and as she toed off her boots in the mudroom she felt ready for a fight and actually *hoped* Jack was nearby.

Then she heard Dianne's voice in her head: *"Don't antagonize him."* That deflated her indignant bubble a bit. She'd be nice if it killed her.

But Jack wasn't around. The kitchen was empty, the sale paperwork still sitting on the counter. The living room was just as empty. She glanced down the hallway, but no light or noise came out of the office either.

Jack's car sat in the driveway, so he hadn't gone far. Of course his room and the gym were on the far side of the house, but she didn't have a good excuse to go wandering down that hallway to see where he was. Plus, she didn't want to take the chance of running into him while he was hot and sweaty and half dressed again. Last night had been bad enough.

For the time being she was alone, and for the first time in a long time she didn't mind the quiet. With her stomach still tied in a knot, eating was out of the question, but a glass of wine sounded like a great plan.

She grabbed a glass and a bottle of last year's Chardonnay and retreated behind her bedroom door.

She still had a lot of thinking to do.

The sun was completely behind the hills and he still hadn't heard Brenna come in. She'd been gone early, too, probably around dawn, because the coffee she'd left in the pot had tasted old when he'd made his way into the kitchen this morning.

The early morning was to be expected; he remembered all too well the rush to get the grapes in before it got too hot—for the grapes, not the people. But sunup to sunset? That meant something had gone wrong at the winery with the crush, and Brenna would be in a bad mood when she finally did make it back to the house.

He wasn't going to concern himself with her mood—beyond the fact it would make any conversation even more difficult than last night's had been. The papers were still on the counter, unsigned, but in a different place than he'd left them, telling him she'd at least looked through them at some point.

He'd spent the day in Max's office, alternating between talking to his secretary and going through the winery's books. He didn't want to leave until he had this settled with Brenna, because he fully intended to never darken the doorway again once he left this time, but he couldn't be away from the city indefinitely. At some point he did need to finish the preparations for his meeting in New York next week. Unfortunately, he hadn't been able to come up with many ideas that would both placate Brenna and sever his ties with this place at the same time.

Dianne Hart, whom he only vaguely remembered as one of Brenna's friends from high school, had brought two plates of dinner to the house late in the afternoon, explaining as she did so that she normally fed Brenna during harvest time, and bashfully explained she'd figured he'd need dinner, too.

She'd chatted to him as she moved easily through the kitchen, balancing a wide-eyed baby on one hip, explaining how she'd moved to Amante Verano five years ago, shortly after Brenna's mother died. When Brenna took her mother's place as vintner, she'd hired Dianne's then newlywed husband Ted as viticulturist. Dianne seemed loyal to Brenna to the core, and had only glowing things to say about her, yet she didn't seem to share Brenna's animosity toward him.

Or if she did, she did a better job of hiding it than Bren. He hadn't missed the way her eyes had strayed to the papers on the counter, though. No doubt Dianne was fully up-to-date on the situation, and he vaguely wondered if Brenna had sent Dianne with instructions to help smooth the path.

But before he could question her, to uncover any underlying motives, she'd been gone. Dianne was Brenna's polar opposite in both looks and temperament, but she had that same earth mother wholesomeness. Years ago that had been part of Brenna's allure—so different from the women he'd grown used to at home. He'd learned his lesson well, though. He'd take Gucci over granola any day.

Boredom and an empty house drove him outside to the pool, where he pulled up short. He'd forgotten how Max had recreated his rooftop retreat at Garrett Tower here—only on a larger scale. White flagstones, warm under his feet, formed the pool deck, while large pots of hibiscus, hellebores and yarrow divided the space, providing secluded seating areas and privacy for the hot tub. Eerie. Almost like being at home.

He swam several laps, then hooked his arms over the edge and listened to the quiet sounds of the evening. Even with the sun down the night was still warm—no need to heat the pool here in the summertime. With nothing more than a few vineyards scattered over the surrounding miles, the lack of light pollution made the stars seem brighter, clearer. A few wispy clouds crossed in front of the rising moon, but no high-rise buildings blocked the view.

This was possibly the only thing he didn't dislike about Amante Verano. When Max had bought the vineyard, *this* was what had first brought Jack out here, not some love of the *vino*.

The French doors to Brenna's bedroom opened, and she stepped quietly onto the patio. Her hair was pulled up and secured with a clip, leaving her profile and the long column of her neck exposed. She drank deeply from a large wine glass as she walked, obviously unaware of his presence, the belt to her short robe trailing behind her on the flagstones. Brenna set the glass carefully on a stone table and shrugged out of the robe.

And then he remembered what else had attracted him to Max's vineyard.

Even in the dim light he could see the defined muscles in her slender shoulders, arms and back—muscles developed from hauling endless bins of grapes, not on some piece of equipment in a gym. The dark bikini didn't cover much, allowing him a sight he hadn't seen in years but had never forgotten. Her body was compact, strong. He knew from experience the power in those thighs, the way the firm muscles covered in soft skin would flex under his hands.

The water, warm just a minute ago, now felt cool against his heated skin, and that old flame sparked to life.

Then Brenna stretched, her back arching gracefully as she lifted her arms over her head, drawing his eyes to the generous curve of her breasts and down the flat plane of her stomach.

And the flame seared through him like a flash fire, fanned by the rush of erotic memories tumbling through his heated brain. He flattened his palms on the pool apron and pushed, heaving himself out of the water.

At the noisy rush of water Brenna spun, the force causing the clip to lose its grip and sending the mass of red hair tumbling around her shoulders. "Jeez, Jack, *when* did you take up skulking in the dark as a hobby?"

He was already reaching for her when her words registered, and he grabbed a towel instead, busying his hands by drying himself off and knotting the towel around his waist in an attempt to camouflage the raging erection she'd caused. "Since when is swimming 'skulking in the dark'?"

"Since you started doing it here." Her hands weren't entirely steady as she gathered her hair and secured it back on top of her head. He felt as well as saw Brenna's eyes move over his chest like a caress, tracking downward until her cheeks reddened. When her eyes flew upward to meet his, he recognized the glow there. It had been a while since he'd seen it, and it stoked the fire burning in him.

Brenna shifted uncomfortably as he returned his slow gaze to her body, and she reached for her robe.

"It's not like I haven't seen it before, Bren. No need to be modest."

Her jaw tightened, but the goad didn't bring a retort. Instead, she stared beyond him into the dark vineyards. The silence stretched out for long minutes as they stood there, until Brenna finally cleared her throat. "If you'd— I mean, are you tr— Um, I'll leave you to it."

"Retreat again, Bren?"

Her shoulders pulled back and settled. "No, no retreat. But I came out here to relax, and fighting with you is not on my list of things I'd like to do tonight."

Images of what *he'd* like to do tonight swam in front of his eyes, and he forcefully shut them out. His body's reaction to Brenna might be beyond his mind's control, but he wasn't a kid anymore. He'd learned his lesson the hard way and, while she was very tempting…

Who was he kidding? He wanted her. Badly. "Don't let me stand in the way of your swim."

"Swim? Oh." She smiled weakly. "I wasn't planning on a swim."

He looked pointedly at her swimsuit. "Interesting choice of attire, then."

Brenna rolled her eyes at him as she reached for her wine glass. "I've had a long day," she said as she stepped around the pots of hellebores and sank into the bubbling hot tub with a sigh. She arched an eyebrow at him. "Do you mind?"

He knew he shouldn't, but he took the opening anyway. "Not at all." He'd dropped his towel and taken the seat opposite her in the hot water before Brenna could stop sputtering. "We have a lot to talk about."

Brenna closed her eyes and sank lower, until the water covered her shoulders. "Not tonight, Jack."

She didn't realize the vineyard was the last thing on his mind at the moment. "Why not?"

"Because I really don't want to fight with you again. It's exhausting, and I'm exhausted enough already."

"Who said we had to fight?"

She opened her eyes, giving him a "get real" look. "We haven't had a civilized conversation in years. You think we'll succeed tonight? Under these circumstances?"

Brenna had a point, but the soft, husky voice had him mesmerized. Even her snappy comebacks lacked any real sarcasm or heat. It boded well. He leaned back, mirroring her position, and shrugged. "So far, so good."

She laughed softly. "Well, there's a first time for everything, I guess."

He was actually suffering from *déjà vu* at the moment. Brenna, quiet if not quite relaxed, the steam rising in wisps around her face, her legs stretched out on the bench only inches from his. His body reacted to the memories, wanting to pull her into his lap...

"How are things with the hotels? Max said you were planning on expanding to the east coast?"

Brenna's question snapped him back to the present. "Everything is going well. I'm headed to New York next week to finalize the deal."

A small smile pulled at the corner of her mouth. "Max would be pleased. He always wanted a hotel in Manhattan."

"And all this time I thought he just wanted a winery." He winked at her, enjoying the look of surprise that crossed her face at the gesture.

"Well, he got that. But you know how Max was always thinking ahead to the next thing."

"Garrett men aren't satisfied easily." He met her eyes evenly, and held the stare until her cheeks flushed and she broke away.

Brenna's eyes traveled over his chest and shoulders hungrily, before she snapped them back up to his face and coughed awkwardly. "They're also hard to please sometimes," she retorted, but she did it with a smile on her face so he couldn't take it as an attack.

Brenna closed her eyes again and sank a little deeper into the water. Her legs brushed against his, and she moved them away quickly. They sat there in silence for a few minutes, and he watched the tension slowly begin to ease from her body. When she finally spoke, her voice was calm and casual again. "We got the last of those grapes in today. It was a really nice yield, and they made gorgeous juice."

Small talk seemed oddly easy at the moment. It certainly beat fighting, and his hopes that this night might turn out to be interesting grew. "Only you would call grape juice gorgeous."

She smiled. "Gorgeous juice makes gorgeous wine. And that makes me very happy indeed."

"What else makes you happy, Bren?" The question came out of nowhere, shocking him almost as much as her.

She sighed tiredly. "Are we going to fight now?"

He couldn't stop the small smile her question caused, but Brenna's eyes were still closed and she couldn't see it. "Not unless you start it. It's a simple question."

Her shoulders sagged. "Fine. Let's see." She thought for a long moment, floating her hands on the water's surface and humming. "Good grapes and good wine."

Did she ever think about anything else? "Besides wine, Bren."

Brenna pursed her lips in mock annoyance. "Um… Walks through the vineyard right at sunset—when it's peaceful and cool, but not dark yet."

They'd been on several memorable sunset walks together, but he didn't think Brenna would appreciate the reminder at the moment.

"Brownie fudge ice cream. And… And… Can I say good wine again?"

"That's not very creative."

That caused her eyes to open again. "What can I say? I have simple needs. What about you?"

He had to think. "Board meetings where no one brings me a disaster to fix. Fast cars. Single-malt Scotch."

Brenna shook her head. "That's a strange list."

"Well, we all can't be blissful just hanging out at Amante Verano making good wine." He shrugged.

He'd said it off-hand, but Brenna's chin dropped and her teeth worried her bottom lip. He knew that look, too, so he waited to see what she was working up the courage to say.

"I'm very sorry, Jack."

An apology? He'd expected a volley about the sale of the winery, or even a statement about Max, designed to play on his sense of duty to the vineyard. Not an apology. What was she angling for? "What for, Bren?"

"A lot of things. But mainly for keeping you away from here."

He snorted, and Brenna looked at him in question. "Brenna, if I'd had any desire to come out here, your presence wouldn't have stopped me."

Confusion wrinkled her forehead. "But you used to love it here—you were out here all the time. It was just after…after, you know, the divorce that you quit coming. I know that was because of me, and I am sorry for that."

Interesting. There were many ways he could respond, but something about Brenna's honesty brought out the same in him. "I don't like wine, I don't like grapes, and I certainly don't have any interest in agriculture of any sort. Think about it—how often did I come out here in the two years after Max bought the property?"

"Maybe twice that I know of…"

He leaned forward and held her gaze. "That's because you were in school and I hadn't met you yet. Then I came out with Max for your graduation…"

Brenna's eyes widened and her jaw dropped. "Are you saying you only came out here to see *me* that summer?"

He nodded, enjoying the waves of shock that moved over her face as she re-aligned her thought processes. "And after we were over there was no reason for me to come back."

CHAPTER FOUR

BRENNA struggled to make sense of his words. The chirp of crickets and the bubbles of the tub's jets covered the sound of her rough, shallow breaths as the ramifications of his simple statement hit home. "I always assumed it was me keeping you away."

Jack shrugged a muscular shoulder, drawing her attention back to his body. Thankfully, much of it was submerged, and no longer quite the magnet for her eyes. Jack in nothing but swim trunks brought back too many memories, and her brain simply couldn't balance both important conversation and gawking at Jack's body at the same time. She struggled to focus on what Jack was saying.

"Why? You knew good and well by the time we got divorced that there wasn't much attraction out here for me."

She'd been the attraction before. That explained some things… "But you didn't even come to see Max after the divorce."

"Staying under the same roof with your ex—especially when your former mother-in-law is sleeping with your father—isn't exactly a tourist attraction." A wry smile crossed his face. "No matter how nice the scenery."

Okay, she knew that. She'd even considered moving back into her old house at the time, only Max and her mom had talked her out of it.

Jack's legs were so close to hers under the bubbling water they rubbed against hers as he shifted position. The brief contact sent a zing through her. But she couldn't hold eye contact, because the smoldering look there wreaked havoc on her insides. If she kept her eyes on his forehead it was easier to concentrate, and she'd be able to keep up with this conversation.

"Then Max started spending even more time out here and less in the city," he continued, as if he didn't know how she was having trouble following along, "and the company took over my life. What little free time I had left I wasn't going to spend it out here, regardless."

Suddenly she realized that for the first time since… well, since the beginning of the end, there was no anger underlying Jack's words. While that absence calmed her guilty conscience, and the part of her that was always so on edge whenever she so much as thought of him, she wasn't deaf to the other heat adding weight to his words. *That* heat her body recognized immediately, even though she hadn't heard it in years. To her great embarrassment her breasts began to tingle and a familiar ache settled in her core.

It was gratifying to know that after everything Jack wasn't completely immune to her. That he didn't hate her enough to make his body forget what had brought them together in the first place. Her skin felt flushed, and she hoped the steam and the hot water would take the blame.

But she couldn't lose focus. This conversation was too important. His concise explanation didn't quite explain as much as his casual demeanor implied. "But Max always…" She stopped herself, unwilling to say the words.

Jack looked at her closely. "You think Max blamed you?"

She nodded. "He had to. He was so disappointed after the divorce."

"Max didn't like having his plans thwarted. He had this whole hotel-slash-winery empire planned, and you managed to accomplish the one thing he couldn't do—made me give a damn about this place. The divorce put him back at zero—at least until he came up with this ridiculous scheme. Max didn't blame you for the divorce, Bren. He saved all the blame for me."

Jack didn't sound bitter, just matter-of-fact. If anything, it made her feel worse about the situation. "Then I'm sorry for that. I'm sorry I caused a rift between you and Max."

"Quit apologizing. You didn't cause anything. You were just a handy excuse."

Just an excuse? No way. "There's got to be more to it than that. Your relationship with Max—"

"Has nothing to do with the current situation." He brushed her words aside with a wave of his hand.

She pulled her legs up to her chest and hugged them. The stress she'd come out here to alleviate was building instead. Hot tub jets were no match for the knots Jack caused, but the stress was much less disturbing than her inappropriate tingling. "Then why? If it's not because of me and it's not because of Max, then *why* do you want to sell so badly?"

She worked up the courage to look at him then, but he didn't look angry. More like resigned and tired of talking about it. "How many times do I have to say it? I don't want to own a winery. I know that's an alien concept for you, because you *do*, but not everyone has a burning desire to make wine. You need to get off the property more. Expand your circle of friends and see there's a whole world out there *not* obsessed with grapes."

There it was. The snide remark. The dismissive tone. She should have known it was coming instead of being lulled by his civility and the intimate atmosphere caused by their surroundings and the conversation. She needed more space, and she pushed herself out of the steaming water. The air felt chilly against her heated skin but did nothing to cool her rising temper. "God, you're such a jerk."

Jack had the nerve to look taken aback. "What now?"

The tingle thankfully disappeared as old resentments bubbled up. This was much easier. "You. Acting so superior and condescending. Little Brenna is so sheltered and naïve, she couldn't possibly know any better."

"You can't deny you've been sheltered out here. You used to admit that readily."

She started to pace in agitation. "Maybe. That

doesn't mean I'm naïve. Just because I never went to college…"

Jack pushed out of the water as well and sat on the edge of the tub. "That was *your* decision. UC Davis would have let you in."

"Only because my last name was Garrett at the time. And why would I spend all that time at school for them to teach me what I already knew about wine-making?"

"You might have enjoyed it. Or you could have gone to a different school and studied something else."

Now a pang of old hurt joined the resentment. "Oh, I'm *so* sorry my lack of formal education was such an embarrassment in front of your snobby city friends."

"Having interests other than grapes makes them snobs?"

"No, looking down on people makes them snobs." She crossed her arms over her chest. "*You* should know from all the practice you've had."

Jack ran his hands through his hair in exasperation. "Why are we having this fight again? We're not married anymore."

And they'd just run through many of the reasons why. *Again.* "Thank goodness for that." She reached for her wine glass and drank deeply.

"If anyone's a snob, Brenna, it's you."

She choked on her wine. "What? Hardly."

Jack stood and walked to within an inch of her. "You're a wine snob. All that 'fruit of the vine, nectar of the gods' garbage. It gets old. And quite boring."

The comment stung, but she stood her ground. "Gee, I'm sheltered, naïve, snobbish *and* boring—and you're an overbearing, condescending jerk with a superiority complex. I don't know how we ever ended up together in the first place."

She regretted the words the moment they left her lips. When would she learn not to wave the red flag in front of the bull just because she was angry?

Jack's eyes lit alarmingly and traced a path down her body, leaving her skin tingling again in their wake. *How* had she forgotten she was practically naked? And that he was, too? Her nipples tightened against the fabric of her bikini, and a slow half-smile crossed Jack's face. "Oh, I think you remember why, Bren," he said quietly. "I know I do."

His husky voice moved through her and every nerve-ending came to life. She was close enough to feel the heat radiating off his body. A rush of desire slammed into her, making her knees wobble and her heart beat faster. Damn him. "D-don't change the subject."

"I'm not. This has always been the subject." He traced a finger over her collarbone and down the top of her arm. Gooseflesh rose up in its wake, and a shiver moved through her. "We've always had this."

"Jack, don't." Her voice sounded breathy and unsteady even to her, but she couldn't pull away from the tease of his touch or the promise in his voice. Her body screamed for more, and all she'd have to do would be to take a tiny step forward...

No. She closed her eyes, blocking the sight of temptation, but her other senses were still under assault and she swayed on her feet. Sex wouldn't solve anything. *It never had*, she reminded herself. They'd been down this path many, many times. Fight bitterly, then have fabulous make-up sex. It never made anything better. In this case it could only make things worse. More complicated.

She *had* to remember that, no matter how much her body begged to differ. No matter how strong the ache was.

No matter how much she wanted him.

She knew what his hands could do to her, remembered the feel of his skin against hers. And from the fire in Jack's eyes she knew he was remembering as well. A tiny shiver of desire rippled through her.

His finger finished its slow path down her arm and now tickled across the sensitive skin of her waist, over her stomach, where butterflies battered her insides.

"Jack, I...I mean *we* shouldn't. Can't." She didn't know exactly what she was trying to say, but weak protest was better than none at all.

Jack's voice rumbled through her. "But we *can*. And you know you want to." The tickling fingers became a warm caress as his palm moved over the dip in her waist to the plane of her lower back.

Be strong. Brenna inhaled, filling her starved lungs with oxygen and the enticing smell that was uniquely Jack. *Now step away.* The signal to her feet to move got lost in transit as Jack's arm began to encircle her.

She was wavering, and she hated herself for it. *What harm could it do?* her body argued.

A lot, her heart responded.

Hundreds of reasons—solid, rational reasons—why this would be a mistake raced through her mind, but that didn't stop her from taking a step closer to him. Jack's fingers tightened on her back, urging her closer still, until she could feel the hairs on his chest tickling faintly across her skin.

Brenna's brain felt foggy, and she lifted her hand to his chest to create a barrier. Jack inhaled sharply at her touch, and the muscle under his skin jumped in response.

Just a taste.

Jack's hand came up to lift her chin, angling it for his kiss, and reality intruded one last time. She'd regret this either way, but which choice would she regret more?

His mouth was almost on hers when she clasped her hand around his wrist. She could feel the heavy beat of his pulse under her fingers, matching the thumping in her chest. Jack's cheek slid across hers as she turned her face away.

"You want me, Bren. I can feel it," Jack whispered.

Oh, he was so right about that. And she could feel how much he wanted her. All she had to do was say yes…

"I'll make this easier for you." Jack kissed her temple, then moved to her ear, his breath sending shivers down her spine. "Give me tonight, and I'll give you the winery."

Jack heard her sharp gasp a second before her hands landed on his chest and pushed him forcefully away from her. Anger hardened her jaw as her fingers flexed, then curled into a fist. Closing her eyes with the effort, she lowered her hand to her side.

When she opened her eyes, the heat blasted him. "Are you *kidding* me?"

Her anger cut through the last of the sensual haze that had snared him and had to have been the source of his offer. The thought of simply giving her the winery *had* crossed his mind briefly, as a quick and easy way out of this unholy mess, but he hadn't entertained it seriously. After all, as Brenna had pointed out, business was built into his DNA, and *giving* one away wasn't exactly approved business practice.

But the offer was out there now, even if he didn't know what had possessed him to make it. "I'm serious, Brenna." He held the stare, watching as Brenna moved from anger, to shock, through disbelief, and finally settled on outrage. He wasn't going to back pedal, not even as he watched the angry flush creep up Brenna's neck as her temper boiled. Even with indignation radiating off her in waves he burned for her. His fingers itched to touch her again, to feel that smooth skin quiver in pleasure and desire. He knew her taste, and the craving was awakened, familiar and frustrating at the same time.

It would give her the excuse she needed to give in to the desire he knew she felt without recriminations in the morning. He'd be able to get Brenna out of his system *and* break their stalemate over the winery at the same time. Win-win all around.

"Oh. My. *God.*" Brenna took another step back, shaking her head in disbelief. As her shoulders tensed, he braced for the full blast of her temper.

But the blow-up didn't come. Her anger seemed to drain away as quickly as it had flared. She moved to the table and perched on the edge, her hands folded against her chin. "I always thought we'd hit every low possible, but this is a new one." Her shoulders slumped as the last of the ire went out of her voice, and she laughed hollowly. "It's a hell of an offer, Jack. Prostituting myself in order to keep my vineyard. It's appropriate, though. I'm screwed no matter what I do."

Put like that, his proposition sounded tawdry, instead of expedient yet pleasurable for them both. "If you want to look at it that way—"

"There's another way?" she scoffed. "If I sign off on the sale I get you out of my life permanently, but I gain God-only-knows-who as a partner, and there's no telling what *that* will do to my business. If I don't sign off on the sale you'll make my life hell in a multitude of interesting ways." Brenna started to pace, her hands moving in agitated circles as she talked. "So I can sleep with you, throwing away what little self-respect I still have, but gaining my business free and clear. In theory, that sounds really great—except I've already told you that I need your name backing me for a while."

She finally faced him, her hands on her hips, her chest heaving under her skimpy bikini top. The anger was back. "Tell me, *exactly* what other way there is to look at it. The way where I'm not screwed, personally *and* professionally?"

Wide-eyed and expectant, she glared at him, waiting for an answer. He didn't have one readily available. He'd backed her into a corner, and she had no graceful means of escape. The professors from his MBA program would be proud—hell, Max would be proud—

of his use of the time-honored strategy of putting his adversary into a position where he definitely had the upper hand in the negotiations.

Except putting Brenna there didn't bring the satisfaction it would in any other situation.

As the silence stretched out Brenna's breathing turned ragged, and he saw the tears gathering in the corners of her eyes. She closed her eyes again and took a deep breath, as if she were trying to pull herself together and hold the tears at bay.

The action stabbed him in the chest, as he'd never seen her tear up before. *Brenna didn't cry.* She exploded, she shouted, she slammed doors, and she even sulked occasionally, but she *didn't cry.*

He'd pushed her too far this time. Considering their past, that was an accomplishment in itself. Their marriage had fallen apart and she'd never shed a single tear. Hell, she'd sat dry-eyed and stoic through her own mother's funeral. But her beloved damn winery brought out the waterworks. Astonishing and insulting, but he still felt like a snake.

Neither of them had a graceful escape route, but he could try to defuse the situation. It wasn't easy—not with his body still wired and ready to finish what he'd started—but he managed a toneless "Forget it, Bren. Chalk the offer up to temporary insanity."

Brenna's eyes flew open, widening in shock as her jaw dropped. She looked as if she'd just been slapped. "What?"

"I said forget it."

"Oh, I don't think so." Brenna's hackles were back

up, but it beat her tears. "You can't toy with me like that and then just walk away. Things have changed, Jack. I won't let you hurt me again."

Where had this come from? "Hurt you?"

"Maybe you can keep things in little boxes, all compartmentalized in your head, but I can't. You can't come out here and turn me inside out and expect me to just take it. You broke my heart once, Jack. I'm finished crying over you."

Her? Heartbroken? Crying? She'd walked out dry-eyed and never looked back. "You left me, Bren. Don't forget that."

Her mouth twisted. "Yes, and you were kind enough to order a ride for me while I packed."

"What, exactly, was I supposed to do? You said you were miserable and that you wanted to go home. I couldn't force you to stay."

"You didn't want me to stay. You were just as miserable as I was."

"Did I ever say that, Bren?"

"You didn't have to." Her voice broke on the last word, and Brenna cleared her throat. "You're right. We should just forget this."

Oh, no, he wasn't going to let Bren retreat. Not after tossing down the gauntlet. "Here's a newsflash for you. *You* left. *You* served me with divorce papers. Don't blame me for your broken heart when you're the one who walked out."

Brenna pulled back as if he'd slapped her. Then her eyes narrowed. "You're saying it was all my fault? Don't even try. It takes two people to make a relationship fail that spectacularly. I loved you, Jack, and it hurt too much that you didn't love me."

Had he heard her correctly? "You think I didn't love you?"

"You *wanted* me." She made it sound distasteful.

"I'm not denying that. But if you want to talk pain and heartache, try your wife telling you she'd rather live at a damn vineyard in Sonoma than with you. We can divvy out blame however you want to for the rest of our problems, but don't try to tell me I didn't love you. Because you'd be wrong."

He was rewarded for his honesty when Brenna's eyes grew wide. She opened her mouth to speak, then closed it again with a snap. "Maybe we were better off when we weren't speaking to each other."

No one could wind him up like Brenna could. This debacle of an evening was proof of that. "I'm inclined to agree with you."

"Then why—?"

"I think we've taken this discussion as far as it can go. No sense circling back and rehashing the past again. When you're ready to sign the sale papers, let me know." Picking up his towel from where he'd dropped it earlier, he draped it over his shoulders and left her standing there, glaring at him.

It certainly wasn't for the first time. Oddly, though, this time he felt as if he deserved it.

Watching Jack walk away was like reliving yet another painful scene from their marriage. Except this time there wouldn't be the fabulous make-up sex later on.

Knees shaking, she made her way carefully to the table and sank into a chair. She heard the door to the house close, and now, safely alone, she let her head drop into her hands. So much had been thrown at her tonight, and she wasn't sure she could process it all.

This was a nightmare—the kind she couldn't wake up from. She'd been so close—too close—to giving in to the sensual pull of Jack that if he hadn't whispered his indecent proposal into her ear at that exact moment she'd probably be happily under him right now.

But to have him offer her… God, it didn't bear thinking about. She didn't know which was worse: the fact Jack thought so little of her now he believed she'd be willing to sell herself for Amante Verano, or the fact she'd seriously considered it for a nanosecond.

And how to explain the pain that had shot through her when he withdrew his offer altogether?

No one could rip her apart with the effortless efficiency of Jack Garrett. She'd thought—make that *hoped*—time and maturity would have made her immune to him. Or that he'd forgotten how.

Tears burned in her eyes. *No*, she told herself angrily as she took deep breaths. She would not cry over him again. She'd long ago grown weary of crying after one of them walked out, and she was finished with that. It had to be the rehashing that had her so close to blubbering again.

She'd loved him so much back then, but over the years she'd decided it had been a one-sided affair. To have him say he'd loved her? To hear that she'd hurt him when she left? That was a one-two punch she hadn't seen coming, and her head was still reeling.

Once upon a time she'd believed her love for Jack could solve anything life threw at them. But the cold reality of their endless cycle of fight-truce-sex-fight had shown her how big the gap between them really was. The inability to bridge that gap had always been her secret failure, the thing she'd never admitted to anyone.

But for a few minutes tonight she'd thought they'd almost built that bridge. She'd briefly felt that old connection—the one they'd had in the very beginning, when they could talk for hours about everything and nothing. That feeling had been buried quickly in the ensuing mess, and she felt a pang of disappointment at the loss.

Brenna sighed and lifted her head. Everything looked exactly the same, seeming to belie the upheaval she'd just gone through. The glowing lights from the pool, the bubbling hot tub, the chirp of the crickets and the smell of the flowers created a serene setting designed to soothe—exactly what she'd come looking for tonight. But it was wasted on her now.

Her insides tumbled over each other and her head ached from the emotional extremes and pressure. Even her wine couldn't calm the storm within her. Grabbing her robe, which she didn't bother putting on, she concentrated on making her shaky legs move her back to the privacy of her bedroom quickly.

Because, damn it, Jack had made her cry. Again.

CHAPTER FIVE

"'EVERY day is a beautiful day at Amante Verano.' Isn't that your motto?" Dianne sing-songed the greeting as she poked her head around the lab door and extended a steaming mug in Brenna's direction.

Brenna accepted the coffee with a grateful smile. After another restless, miserable night, the heady aroma of Di's high-octane brew was a welcome jolt to her sluggish system. "Ever since you printed it on my coffee mug it is."

"Then why do you look like someone kicked that puppy you claim you're going to get?"

She wouldn't be able to avoid this conversation for long. She might as well go ahead and get it over with. "One guess."

"Jack." Dianne pushed a rack of vials and testing supplies to the back of the counter and pulled herself up to sit, her legs swinging gently. "Are you two still fighting? Come on, Brenna, surely there's a better way to sort this out?"

"I wish. Every conversation—no matter how nice I try to be—always deteriorates into a shouting match.

And last night was a nightmare. I thought exes were supposed to get more civil as time progresses. Not us." Brenna shook her head and leaned back in her chair.

"Unfinished business, I think."

Brenna stared into her coffee. "I don't know what you mean."

Dianne snorted. "Try that with someone who didn't witness the whole thing. I watched you fall goofy-stupid in love, elope, and then divorce in less than six months. I also know what that did to you—even if you tried to hide it from everyone else."

Her stomach was hollow enough at the moment. She didn't need Dianne making it worse. "Where's Chloe?" she asked with forced cheerfulness.

"With her father, learning the intricacies of wine-making, testing and probably teething on your new digital refractometer. Now, don't change the subject." She shook her head in disappointment. "It was a weak attempt, anyway. No points for effort."

"I thought it might work there for a minute," Brenna grumbled.

"With someone else, maybe. But you can't fool me. Now, spill. What is going on with you two?"

She certainly wasn't going to go into detail. She still hadn't made sense of it yet herself. "You know the basics. Then, last night, Jack offered to *give* me his half of the winery."

Dianne lit up and she clapped her hands. "That's fantastic! It's not perfect, I know, but it beats…" She trailed off as Brenna shook her head slightly. "Oh, no. There's a 'but,' isn't there? I hate the 'but.'"

"No 'but.' An 'if.'"

Dianne's forehead wrinkled in confusion. "I'm not following you. An 'if'? What kind of 'if'?"

Brenna glanced over to make sure the lab door was firmly closed. "Jack offered to give me his half *if*—" She took a deep breath. "*If* I slept with him."

Her eyes widened. "You're not serious?" Brenna nodded, and Dianne's jaw dropped. "That's—that's—that's…"

"Disgusting? Amoral?" she offered. "Brilliant? Good business sense? I honestly don't know."

"But you didn't." Di looked at her carefully. "*Did* you?"

"No! Do you think I'd be in this bad shape if I was now sole owner?" Brenna leaned back in the chair and took another sip of coffee. "I have to admit, though, it was pretty tempting." And if she'd given in to that temptation she wouldn't have been turned inside out by the rest of their conversation.

"And I can see why. You get everything you want just for a little nookie? That's a helluva return on your investment." Brenna felt her own eyebrows go up at the words, and Dianne cleared her throat. "Not that you would, though. That would be wrong."

"I had no idea you had such a practical Machiavellian streak. In some ways it does seem like a relatively minor thing to do—I mean, it's not like I've never had sex with him before."

"Ah-ha!" Dianne jumped off the counter. "*That's* what was tempting you. Not the vineyard. Oh, no. Sex with Jack again was the temptation."

That much was true. No sense in lying. "Yes. Jack was the temptation. I haven't forgotten what it was like. I remember every single detail." Images danced through her memory, bringing a physical response. *"Vividly."*

"So do I, and I only heard them from you," Di said, fanning herself.

"But I'm not stupid. Physically and financially it sounds like a pretty decent deal, but honestly—and if you repeat this I'll kill you—I'm afraid it would hurt too much. In here." She placed a hand over her chest.

"Afraid you wouldn't be able to respect yourself in the morning?"

"That, too." She'd come to several conclusions in the wee hours of the morning. Including that one.

"Ahh." Dianne bit her lip. She understood. "Jack still has a piece of you. I suspected as much."

"I don't know how or why, but, yeah, it seems he does. You'd think I'd be over him by now. It's been a long time."

"Avoidance doesn't mean you've been dealing."

"I guess not. Now look at me." Brenna balanced her elbows on her knees and let her head rest in her hands. "I'm a mess. And I'm *in* a hell of a mess."

"That explains a lot of the fighting." Dianne returned to her perch on the counter and drummed her nails on it.

"What do you mean by that?"

"Unfinished business, remember? Maybe Jack has some, too."

"Oh, please." Jack didn't sound like someone with unfinished business—unless she counted the winery, of course. "You're insane. And that noise is making *me* insane."

Dianne stopped the drumming and folded her hands in her lap. "Jack doesn't need to bribe or blackmail women to get them to sleep with him. There's got to be a reason he propositioned you."

Her heart skipped a beat. She'd thought about that, too, and decided not to dig too deep lest she find something to make her even worse off than she already was. "I have to admit, though, it's the one thing we were really good at. It was everything else that didn't work."

"Still…even good sex can't be that hard for him to come by. There are lots of women in San Francisco, and he's rich, young, and unbelievably handsome. He doesn't need to hit you up for ex-sex for a little relief."

Pulling her hair out sounded like a grand plan about now. "*Argh*. Can we pick another subject now? Please?"

"Just one more question." Dianne turned serious. "What are you going to do?"

"I don't know. I don't think the offer is open now anyway—not after last night's blowout. I may sound like a broken record, but I just don't *know*."

"You'll figure it out. I know you will." Dianne left her then, squeezing her shoulder in comfort and support as she passed Brenna's chair. Dianne also left the Thermos of coffee for her, but her stomach didn't seem stable enough to take more.

Brenna stared at the walls—old pictures, notes written in her mother's elegant handwriting, label prototypes, newspaper clippings and lists of local growers all competed for space. She would figure it out. She had to. But last night's revelations wouldn't leave her alone.

She'd loved Jack, but he'd also offered an excitement

she'd lacked living out here on the property. When that had gone to hell she'd slunk home, to the one place where she understood who and what she needed to be. She'd thrown herself into Amante Verano—partly because she loved it, but also partly to fill the gap losing Jack had created.

Right or wrong, though, this was her life now. Everything she'd worked for in the last ten years had come to this moment. Jack's presence had just created a wrinkle; the blast from her past shaking her world a little. She needed to come to a workable arrangement with Jack, and once she did everything would go back to normal.

And Jack himself... Well, she needed to get past old hurts and old feelings and remember what they were *now*—not what they had been. All she had to do was ignore that pull he had on her and take back that little piece of her he still seemed to have. Needless to say sleeping with Jack was out of the question. *For any reason*, she told herself.

In the meantime, sitting around moping in frustration wasn't going to change anything—at least she knew *that* much. She also had a to-do list a mile long, and she wouldn't accomplish any of it hiding out in her lab.

Her first stop was the storeroom, where the banal task of inventory was waiting for her. Before she could get started, though, her cellphone rang. Fishing it out of her back pocket, she checked the number. What could Di want?

"Where's Jack?"

She eyeballed the boxes containing bottles, mentally calculating. "At the main house, I assume."

"No, because I'm at the main house. His car's gone."

Brenna's heart jumped in her chest, then sank. Which is it? she asked herself. Am I happy or not? "Gone?"

Di sounded exasperated. "I can't believe he'd take off without telling anyone. That's just plain rude. And after what you said about last night…"

It *was* a bit of a slap in the face. "Jack can come and go as he pleases. He doesn't owe anyone any kind of explanation."

"Maybe he just went into town for something. Want me to check his room and see if his stuff's gone? It would give us a clue if he's planning on coming back or not."

"Di, no. If he's not coming back he'll call. Or have his lawyer call. It's not like anything is settled. We should enjoy the break while we can."

Then why didn't she feel any relief? She still felt the tightness around her chest that hurt when she breathed. *Good thing I didn't sleep with him.*

"But Brenna…"

"Don't you have something you need to do? Something useful?"

"Fine." Dianne grumbled. "But I wonder where he went? And why?"

Me, too. "It's not our business."

She wasn't naïve enough to believe Jack had simply given up and gone home, and the knots in her stomach tightened. No, Jack had something cooking, and she wasn't going to like it.

"You're off your game. That's the closest I've come to beating you in five years." Roger bounced the blue ball in his direction and Jack caught it easily. "Whatever it is, keep it up. I could get used to not having my ass handed to me twice a week."

Roger's words echoed in the enclosed court as he wiped a towel across his sweaty face. Jack took aim, then sent the ball flying down the court to bounce off the wall and hit Roger in the leg. "I'll never be *that* off my game."

But Roger was right. He was distracted. Two days of dealing with Brenna and he couldn't even keep his mind on a racquetball game. He couldn't decide which was more of a distraction, though: remembering the feel of her skin and the way she'd reacted to his touch, or the look on her face when she accused him of breaking her heart.

"I have three ex-wives, remember?" Roger continued as he packed up his gear. "As your attorney and your friend, I can tell you it never gets any better. The path of least resistance is your best bet. Expensive, but expedient. If you want to stay sane, that is."

"I think I've figured that out for myself." Jack opened the door and stepped out into the cool air of the gym. Brenna had been up and gone before he'd left the house this morning, so he had no idea how she was handling everything that had happened last night.

He'd finally figured out what he wanted around three o'clock this morning, and having a plan had allowed him to finally sleep a little. The erotic dreams of Bren awaiting him had been nice, but the memory of those dreams was definitely a distraction this morning.

"That's a shame. I was looking forward to stomping on you in the near future."

Jack shrugged as Roger fell into step beside him and they headed for the locker room. He had a three o'clock meeting, and he needed to put in a couple of hours at the office before he headed back to Sonoma.

"You know, investing in a winery sounds interesting."

Jack stopped. "Good Lord, not you, too? It's like an epidemic. Everywhere I turn, someone wants to own a winery."

Roger grinned. "Except you, for some reason."

"Because I have no romantic notions about winemaking." Jack returned the greetings of the socialites at the juice bar, and got moving again before any of them decided to come over and say hello in person. He didn't have time—or the inclination at the moment—to deal with that.

Roger trotted to catch up. "Come on, how difficult could it be? Stomp a few grapes, mingle with the tourists, drink a lot. Sounds like a sweet job to me."

Jack spared a glance to see if Roger was kidding. Shockingly, Jack didn't think he was. "When was the last time you were in a vineyard?"

"I took the tour a couple of years ago, when the last set of in-laws visited."

Maybe Bren was right about not selling to just anyone. "And that makes you an expert, of course. Trust me, Brenna would cheerfully and painfully remove your feet if you put them anywhere near her precious grapes."

Roger spun the dial on his locker casually. "I'm surprised you're being so generous. Brenna Walsh must really love you."

That stopped him in his tracks. "What?"

Backtracking, Roger sputtered. "I mean, you're the best ex-husband a woman could ask for. She can't be cursing your name too often."

He doubted that. Brenna was probably burning him in effigy right now.

"You're setting a bad precedent for the rest of us," Roger continued.

Jack closed his locker with a satisfying bang. "Tell you what. You deal with your ex-wives, and I'll deal with mine."

Roger put his hands up and backed away. "Fine. I'll have the papers on your desk this afternoon."

Good. He'd have them in hand when he went back to Amante Verano tonight. He'd use the weekend to go through the rest of Max's things and get Brenna on board with the new plan. By Monday this whole situation would be off his plate and his life could go back to normal.

As the hot water of the shower kneaded his muscles, he realized there was still one last possible problem with his plan. Was Brenna over last night's debacle yet, or was she nursing her anger today, building steam to go another round or two? The fight, the rehashing of the past—it all left a bad taste in his mouth, but it didn't dampen the fire in his blood. Remembering Brenna's physical response only fanned it. He'd reacquainted himself with the way she smelled and the feel of her skin. If he'd just kept his big mouth shut...

Grimacing, he turned the water to cold and pushed the image of Brenna—deliciously wet and covered only in a scrap of fabric—from his mind. He had a lot of real work to do today, and a raging erection wasn't going to help.

Concentrating on the zoning issues for the new property in Sacramento *did* help, and while he might have been · slightly distracted during the endless meetings, he managed to keep Brenna off his mind for the better part of the afternoon.

As promised, Roger's courier had the documents on his desk before the end of the business day, and Brenna was once again front and center in his thoughts. Only this time it was the image of Brenna, teary-eyed and trying to hold it together, that kept appearing.

Brenna had said she was finished crying for him. And she'd said it so candidly, without any other pretense; he was leaning toward believing it. Had she cried alone? Without him knowing?

That would make him a first-class bastard who deserved to have her walk out on him.

Yet another reason he needed out of this mess. Quickly. He should let Roger handle it from here. It would be easier on him and Brenna both.

Then why the hell was he on his way to Sonoma?

Because I want her. Brenna was like a bad habit he'd thought he'd kicked years ago, but one tiny taste was enough to awaken the craving. Last night had cleared the air a little about their past, and the papers he had on the seat next to him should take care of their present problem. If Brenna wasn't holding a grudge, he planned to finish what they'd started last night.

As he made the turn onto Amante Verano property he was cautiously optimistic about the night ahead. But, like a junkie who knew his fix was just moments away, the craving intensified as he parked next to Brenna's Jeep.

The low hum of the television greeted him as he opened the door, and he saw Brenna on the couch, her long legs stretched out across the cushions. A magazine lay open on her lap; her face was serious as she read. She toyed with a lock of hair that had escaped the loose twist on the back of her head, more relaxed than he'd seen her in a long time. The image disappeared, though, when she heard his steps on the marble floor and the thud of his briefcase landing on the table. Startled, she turned to find the source of the noise, and the magazine slid to the floor.

"Jack! I—I—didn't realize you'd be back tonight." She pushed a button on the remote and the TV went black.

"Is that a problem?"

"No, not at all. I've already told you you're welcome here." Brenna sounded friendly enough, but he still approached with caution, picking the magazine up off the floor and handing it back to her. It was a wine magazine. No surprise there.

"Interesting reading?"

"Very much so." She grinned at him and his stomach tightened a bit. "There's a fascinating article on cap management regimes, if you are looking for some light reading."

Bren wasn't poised for attack; in fact he almost believed her attitude was genuine. Was she looking for a ceasefire as well? That would make this evening—and all his plans—much easier. "I'll pass, thanks." He took the chair opposite the couch and noticed the glass on the table between them. No stem. Straight sides. A dark amber liquid with a small film of white bubbles across the surface. "Is that a *beer*?"

Brenna laughed. "Yes, it's beer. Dianne and I went to town this afternoon, and I was able to replenish the supplies. Help yourself. There's actual food in there, too, if you're hungry," she called at his back as he headed to the fridge.

Brenna's amazing attitude adjustment seemed too good to be true. His optimism grew.

"A beer is all I need. It's been a hell of a day." He twisted off the cap and held the bottle by the neck as he slid the new agreement out of his briefcase.

"Sorry to hear that. Something wrong at the office?"

Her attempt at small talk brought a smile to his face, and it was tempting to just take his beer back to the living room for the simple, normal activity of human company and conversation after a long day. But that would only be a stalling tactic, and he wanted to get business out of the way first.

Brenna still wore her open, friendly look as he returned to the living room, but it faded as she saw the papers in his hand. Her eyes narrowed. "I'm not signing that."

"You should really read it before you decide." He handed it to her and reclaimed his seat, stretching his legs out in front of him and drinking from the bottle as she flipped through the pages.

"This looks like it could take a while. How about you give me the abridged version instead?" She reached for her own glass, placing the papers on the table and leaving them there as she settled back against the cushions and looked at him expectantly.

"All right. Short version it is. This gives you an additional twenty-five percent share in the business." Her eyebrows went up. "Free and clear," he assured her. "That gives you a majority stake, no matter what happens. In return, you agree to the sale of my remaining twenty-five percent to Garrett Properties, and the company will back you as a silent partner for the next year. At the end of that year you agree to allow the company to sell its interest to whatever buyer it finds— you, of course, will have the right of first refusal at that time, but you cannot block the sale."

"You'd give me another twenty-five percent?" She sounded as if she was waiting for the trap to snap shut. She picked up the papers and began scanning, obviously looking for the catch. "Why?"

Roger had asked him the same question, so he recycled his answer. "Consider it part of your divorce settlement. Half of my half."

"But I didn't get a divorce settlement. We weren't married long enough."

"Then this gives me the opportunity to rectify that lack." Brenna shot him a distrusting look. "Don't look at me like that. It's a gift. No strings beyond what I've already said."

She flipped through a few more pages before placing them back on the table. Picking her glass up again, she stared at the liquid, her eyebrows knitting together as she thought. He could almost see the wheels turning in her head, but he had no idea what conclusions she was drawing.

"I know it's not what you want, but it's the best I can do for you, Bren."

She nodded and drummed her nails on the side of the glass. Then she swallowed hard and lifted her brown eyes to his. "I know it is. And it seems more than fair."

CHAPTER SIX

BRENNA'S throat felt tight. It was *very* fair. More than she could have hoped for, actually. Jack looked shocked. What had he expected? It wasn't as if she had much room to bargain. In fact *she* was shocked he'd been so accommodating. He could have just continued to hound her until she gave in. Because, though she hadn't admitted it to anyone, deep down she'd known she would have eventually buckled under the pressure.

"You agree to those terms?" Jack seemed a little surprised at her easy acceptance.

She nodded and drank deeply from her glass, hoping the beer would loosen the constriction around her vocal cords. It didn't.

Jack sat back in his chair and folded his hands across his stomach. "I'm glad to hear it. There's no sense dragging this out endlessly."

He was being mighty friendly for someone who'd gone ten rounds with her the night before. And this offer, coming out of nowhere like a gift from the gods… What was the catch? Stealth maneuvers and shady business weren't Jack's style at all, though. Maybe there wasn't a catch. "I agree. I assume, though, you won't object if I have my attorney read this before I sign."

"Don't you trust me?" His lips twitched in amusement.

She snorted. "Based on what? Our long, happy history?"

Jack tilted his head, acknowledging the truth to her statement, and shrugged.

"What's the saying? 'Trust, yet verify'? I think on something this important, I should be sure I know exactly what I'm signing."

"That's a sound plan, Bren. But since there's no trapdoors to worry about, I look forward to hearing from your lawyer sometime next week." He raised his bottle in a small toast. "To equitable solutions."

"I'll drink to that." She drained her glass with the toast. Oddly enough, the knots of tension in her stomach finally released a little. After being tied up for so long, the relief felt alien.

Although she did fully intend to go over that agreement with a microscope to be sure, she realized she trusted Jack enough to believe it said what he claimed. She was just glad to have the end of this nightmare in sight.

And it felt really good, even if her hands were still shaking from making a stand.

Jack turned up his bottle and drained it as well. "Another?" he asked as he stood and crossed behind her to the kitchen.

"Please." She heard glass clinking, and the tiny *psfft* as Jack opened the bottles. Maybe she should choose something a bit stronger. It wasn't late, by any stretch of the imagination, but if Jack was starting his second beer it meant he didn't plan on heading back to the city tonight. As he settled back into his seat Brenna realized he might decide to spend the evening in here. With her.

Last night's events were too fresh to ignore, and the memories came back in a disturbing rush of sensation and emotion. Goosebumps formed on her skin as she remembered the feel of his fingers teasing over her stomach, and the sincere shock in his eyes when she had accused him of not loving her. She closed her eyes, only to be met with a vision of water tracing down Jack's chest in the dim patio lights. She quickly opened her eyes and focused on the painting on the far wall as she took deep breaths. The room felt overly warm, and the beer she gulped didn't help cool her any.

Maybe she should go grab the bottle of port. Dull the edges a bit with something more fortified—and forti-fying—than beer.

"No big plans for your Friday night?" Jack asked, snapping her back to the present.

Conversation. Focus on the conversation. "This is it. We lack a happening club scene out here. Much to my dismay, of course." Jack snorted, and took another sip of his beer. "But I could ask you the same thing." She was a happy homebody, while Jack was a social creature—and a popular one, she knew. His life was usually one exciting event after another; surely he had something better to do on a Friday night.

"Well, I'd planned to have a shouting match with you tonight, but it seems like that's been shot down." He winked at her. "Not that I mind, of course, but it has freed up my evening unexpectedly."

"I could throw some insults at you anyway, if you'd like," she offered, in what she hoped was a helpful, teasing tone. It would certainly help *her* keep her mind away from dangerous places. At the same time, though, it was nice not to be at daggers drawn with him.

"Pass." Jack stared out through the French doors at the dark vineyard, and she wondered what he was thinking about. It was easier, though, than having him look at her, and she was glad for the reprieve. The house normally seemed so big and empty, but with Jack here she felt slightly claustrophobic.

How could he look so relaxed? Feet propped up, settled back comfortably in her second favorite chair, he looked very much like the monarch of the glen as he casually lifted the bottle to his lips. His throat worked as he swallowed, calling her attention to the unbuttoned collar of his shirt, where the crisp white cotton looked stark against his tanned neck and the dark hair that just brushed the collar.

She knew what it felt like to run her fingers over the hard muscles at the nape of his neck and thread them through the inky softness—he'd worn it longer when he was younger, and she remembered how it had tickled her skin like a silky caress...

"Don't you get lonely out here, Bren?"

She jumped as he spoke, and felt the guilty flush rise up her neck again. Thankfully, Jack was still focused on the vineyard; maybe he hadn't noticed her inappropriate stare. "Don't you mean bored?" she challenged, out of habit.

"No, I meant lonely." There was no sarcasm in his voice, and when he did turn to look at her she only saw sincere curiosity on his face.

She regretted her snark instantly. "A little. It's been tough since Max died—being alone, that is. The house is awfully big for just one person." She shrugged and stared into her glass, wishing for another beer. "I've been thinking about getting a puppy, though. I could use the company."

Jack seemed to read her mind, and he made the short trek to the kitchen and returned with another bottle for them both. She skipped the glass this time, and held her own bottle by the neck as she drank. Drinking this much this fast was going to give her one hell of a headache tomorrow, but she needed the balm for her nerves.

Instead of returning to his seat, Jack pulled a cushion off the chair and tossed it to the floor beside the couch. As he lowered himself to the floor, he asked, "Do you mind? My back's a little tight from my racquetball game today and the drive back."

"Be my guest." She shifted on the couch, turning to her side to face him more easily in his new position. Jack closed his eyes and stretched, and Brenna's pulse kicked up as she watched. *Keep the conversation going.* She cleared her throat. "Yeah, a puppy. Something big, like a Boxer or a Rottweiler."

Jack smiled without opening his eyes. "And to think you wanted that little Corgi puppy before."

"We lived in a suite in a hotel." A dark eyebrow went up. "Okay, so it wasn't exactly a shoebox apartment, but still, it didn't seem fair to a bigger dog to not have a yard." Jack's grin was heartstopping. She'd forgotten what it was like. "Maybe I'll get two. They can keep each other company. Play together."

"Then who will play with you?" he asked softly.

Her heart skipped a beat and she reached for her drink again. "It's not like I'm a hermit out here. I've got Dianne and Ted and the baby—not to mention the people who work here every day."

"And that's enough for you? You don't have any other…uh…company?"

Shc nearly choked on her drink. She swallowed and coughed painfully. "Are you seriously asking me about my love-life?"

Jack shrugged—a strange movement, considering his position. "I have to admit, I'm a bit curious."

"You should have asked me that before you propositioned me last night."

Jack's eyes popped open, and she saw a strange light there in the dark blue depths. "Probably," he answered, and she realized too late she'd said that last thought aloud.

Damn it, she should have stopped after her second beer. Now her liquor-loosened tongue had taken her smack into the middle of the one topic she'd desperately wanted to avoid. "Just forget it."

He levered himself into a sitting position, putting him a little too close for Brenna's comfort. Those broad shoulders were only inches from her. "I'm finding that difficult to do."

She mustered her bravado, but it was still shaky from Jack's simple proximity. "Guilty conscience?"

"Not at all. I didn't say anything that wasn't true."

She thought of his fingers trailing over her collarbone. *We've always had this.* She fought back the shiver. "And you don't think your little 'bargain' was crass in any way?"

He didn't even have the decency to look the least bit chagrined. Instead, he seemed to be fighting back a smile. "It may have lacked finesse, but my motives were clear."

"Once more for old times' sake?" Her voice shook, completely destroying the casual tone she was hoping for.

"Is that really such a shocker, Bren? The pool, the moonlight… Are you denying it stirred up some fond memories for you, too?"

"Emphatically." She just needed to keep reminding herself of that.

"You're a bad liar. I was there, remember? I had my hands on you. I felt the way you shivered when you re-membered exactly how good we were together."

"In bed, maybe. But I also remember the rest of our, ahem, 'conversation' last night. That also brought back memories—not all of them fond ones."

"We had some good times. You can't deny that." His hand came up to play with her hair.

"Not enough to tip the balance." She shuddered as his hand moved to her face. "We said—and did—some pretty horrible things to each other."

He shrugged away months of arguments and years of pain with "We were young. I'm not carrying a grudge. Are you?"

"From then? Or now?" she countered, mainly to

keep him talking. She couldn't pull away, but this was moving into dangerous territory.

"Ten years is a long time to carry a grudge." His eyes searched her face and she shivered. "Me? I'm grudge-free."

"Then, here's to putting the past behind us. Should we drink to that?" *Anything* to put a little distance between them.

Jack shook his head slightly. He tucked a lock of hair behind her ear, then traced his fingers over the curve of her jaw. "Beautiful. Tempting. Stubborn."

He was close—too close—his face only inches from hers. The gentle caress over sensitive skin and his husky, seductive voice sucked her in, while those blue eyes captured her and led her straight into temptation.

And she desperately wanted to go. Every nerve in her body screamed for Jack to touch her. Her skin begged for it. She'd suffered the aftermath of last night all day—the achy need, the smoldering want. Her mouth went dry as Jack's hand curved around the nape of her neck and his thumb smoothed over the tense muscles.

Just one more time. Do you think you'll ever get this chance again? Once her signature was on those papers, she'd have no reason to see Jack again. That thought put a strange hollow feeling in her chest—one that felt oddly familiar, yet strange, because until yesterday she would have sworn she was long over him.

Jack reached up to remove the clip holding her hair back, and his fingers threaded through the mass to massage her scalp. She closed her eyes in bliss as the tension drained out of her, only for it to be replaced with an aching need. When she opened her eyes again she met Jack's stare, and gasped at the hunger and promise she saw there.

She was lost and she knew it. She always was when Jack looked at her like that. Anger, bruised pride, indignant huffs—none of it was able to stand firm against the need and desire he could fire in her.

Jack seemed to know the moment she made up her mind, and he surged to his knees, pulling her to him and covering her mouth with his.

Yesss. Oh, *yes.*

It wasn't gentle. Or nostalgic or sweet. Jack met her hunger head-on and returned it, his mouth devouring hers. His fingers tightened in her hair, holding her head still as his tongue slid over hers, and she shivered in response.

Jack broke the kiss, sliding his mouth over her jaw to the sensitive skin of her neck. She panted, gasping for air as his teeth grazed her, and she tilted her head back to allow him greater access even as her fingers threaded through his hair to hold him there.

She hadn't forgotten this, but the memory was bland compared to the reality. She groaned, and Jack echoed the sound before his arms locked around her waist and he pulled her off the couch and into his lap.

The feel of Jack's hard body against hers as she straddled his thighs sent tremors through her insides, and she pressed into him, craving the heat and pressure. She pulled at his shirt, bunching it into her hands until she could reach underneath to feel the smooth planes of muscle on his back.

Jack's hot mouth traced her collarbone as his hands slid over her hips to her waist, and finally her ribs, where his thumbs could stroke teasingly against the undersides of her breasts. Her nipples tightened with anticipation and she arched back in invitation.

Instead, Jack pulled her close, his mouth covering hers again, his hands snaking under the hem of her shirt and sliding it up with agonizing slowness. He broke the kiss to sweep the fabric over her head, then gently leaned her back, supporting her with one hand while the other grazed gently over the expanse of her chest and in the valley between her aching breasts.

Brenna shivered, enjoying the tease of his touch yet hating the delay. She was on fire, needing more of him—*all* of him—before the anticipation killed her. One finger circled her nipple, causing her to clench her thighs around his as the pleasure rippled through her. The corner of Jack's mouth turned up in pleasure at her response as he drove her slowly insane with his feather-light touch.

Brenna concentrated on her shaking hands, reaching for the buttons of his shirt. Clumsily, she managed to work them through their holes, pausing occasionally to bite her lip when Jack's slow, deliberate torture became too much. Finally, she pushed the shirt off his shoulders, and his chest was hers to touch.

She echoed his movements, running her fingertips over the ridge of his pecs, teasing his nipples with her nails. His fingers tightened on her waist when he shuddered in pleasure.

A split second later Jack flipped her to her back, her

head landing on the cushion he'd used earlier, and his body finally covered hers. She moaned at the sensation of skin against skin, at the heat and weight of his body nestled in the vee of her legs. How could she have forgotten this? The memories paled in comparison to the reality. How had she ever walked away from this? Jack's kiss sent her head spinning, but when his head dipped lower to capture her nipple between his lips fireworks exploded behind her eyes and she groaned his name.

The sound seemed to spur him, and he suckled harder, causing her to nearly arch off the floor as pleasure shot through her. When his weight shifted off her, she reached for his waist to pull him back, but let her hand fall away when she felt the snap of her shorts release and the zipper give way.

Her stomach tightened under his hand as it slid low and his fingertips tickled along the edge of her panties, while Jack's mouth returned to hers for a shattering kiss. But one rational thought surfaced and made a weak, last-ditch effort: *This is the point of no return. Are you sure?*

Her body answered first, twisting toward him, granting access, but Jack seemed to hesitate briefly, his kiss gentling as if he knew she was fighting one last battle against herself.

Yes.

She knew what Jack could do to her body; the guaranteed pleasure awaiting her. But she'd been faced with the hard fact today that she wasn't as immune to him as she'd long assumed, and deep down she knew she'd be setting herself up for a bad fall in the morning, when Jack walked out of her life again.

Was it worth the risk?

Then Jack pushed the thin silk aside, and his fingers found her heated, needy center. Flames licked through her, leaving her panting against his kiss.

Oh, yes.

Jack felt the last of the uncertainty leave her body just as her thighs clamped around his hand and she shuddered in pleasure. He felt as if he was holding a live wire, and each little sound, every gasp, every tremor, zinged through him like raw electricity.

The need to taste her, to take her, bordered on painful—even more so than the pressure against his zipper—but Brenna was already on the brink. She tore her mouth away and buried her face in his shoulder, muffling low, guttural noises. Brenna's nails bit into his arms, holding him in place while she moved restlessly against his hand and he took her over the edge.

She was still throbbing around his finger when she lifted her face to his. Her cheeks were flushed, but her brown eyes were clear and burning—for *him*. Oh, no, his Bren wasn't done yet; she was still on fire. And, while he'd seen that look before and had even expected it, the raw hunger there slammed into him, causing his breath to catch.

Brenna held his gaze as she released his arm and smoothed her fingers over the half-moon marks her nails had left. Then she lifted her hips, sliding her shorts and panties off and kicking them away quickly. A second later she released his zipper and grasped his straining erection.

She moved so quickly she was an erotic blur, but at the feel of her hot hand on him he exhaled sharply, and closed his eyes to savor the sensation. Brenna had never been a meek partner, but there was an urgency behind her desire this time. He could feel it—in her heated touch, in the desperate movement of her lips, and through the maddening press of her body against his.

He could relate. The same knife-edge cut through him.

When his hand cupped her breast again she hissed and rolled to her back, pulling him over her.

"Now, Jack," she whispered, her breath hot against his ear.

He wanted to slow her down, to savor the feel and taste of her, relearn her skin, but the desperate *"Please…"* she added had him adjusting her hips, parting her thighs, and driving into her so hard he saw stars.

Brenna's back bowed, nearly lifting her completely off the rug, and her fingers dug into his biceps for support. A sheen of moisture covered her body, and he could see the tiny trembles already moving through her. Her tight, throbbing warmth was sanity-snatching, and his hips moved of their own accord.

As he eased slowly out Brenna's head snapped up, her eyes connecting with his as her legs locked around his waist. Gathering her close to his body, he shifted his weight to his elbows and met her halfway as she thrust against him.

He held Brenna's stare as they rocked together, until her eyes glazed over and she buried her face in his shoulder again. He felt the nip of her teeth against his skin as short, sharp cries told him she was falling over the edge. Then Brenna tensed against him, shaking violently with the power of her orgasm. The sensation took him over with her and he groaned as he collapsed on top of her.

It took a long time for reality to return, and when it did it came in pieces. The delicious weight of Jack covering her. The scratch of the wool rug against her back. The sound of Jack's breathing evening out next to her ear. The thump of Jack's heart against her chest. The lovely languorous feeling only a truly mind-scrambling orgasm could provide.

And Jack was the only one who'd ever been able to scramble her mind like that.

Jack had been right about one thing: no matter what else, they'd always had this. She stroked the back of his head absently, loving the silky feel of his hair between her fingers.

Jack stirred. Pushing himself up onto his elbows, he brushed the hair back from her face before leaning in to give her a slow, stirring kiss. Then his lips curled into a breath-stopping smile. "Better?"

She felt her face heat. He'd seen—and felt—that edge of her desperation. She tried to match his smile and act casual. "Oh, yeah. I'm feeling much better now."

"Good." He kissed her forehead, rolled off, and pushed to his feet. He looked like a god standing over her—all golden-skin and lean muscle. She could stare at him forever and never get tired of the view. She let her eyes trail appreciatively over his body before meeting his amused eyes.

He extended his hand and she took it, letting him pull her up. A moment later her feet were swept out from under her, and she found herself pressed against Jack's chest.

But Jack didn't turn in the direction of the hallway to her room, or toward the kitchen and the far side of the house where his room was. Instead, he moved toward the French doors.

"Where are you taking me?" she asked.

"The hot tub."

CHAPTER SEVEN

WAKING up with a warm male body snuggled around her should feel...alien, or wrong somehow. But it didn't. Neither did the strong hand idly caressing her breast, nor the erection pressing insistently against her backside. It felt almost right.

The idle caress turned purposeful, with Jack's thumb grazing across her nipple and sending a shiver through her. Correction, she thought, it felt amazing.

"'Bout time you woke up," Jack murmured against her shoulder. His hand changed course, sliding over her stomach and between her legs.

She hummed in pleasure and parted her thighs to give him better access. Was there a better way to greet a Saturday morning? Weekend mornings had always been her favorite time when they were married. Jack hadn't had to jump up and rush off to work or class, and the whole morning had been theirs to laze in bed, drink coffee, and make love without any pressure to do anything else. She smiled as the first small shudder moved through her. How many times had he awoken her just like this?

Jack's fingers were magic, slowly building the pressure until her hands were fisted in the sheets and her breath became labored. She moaned his name as she started to shatter, and she vaguely heard him encouraging her on with hot words in her ear.

She reached for him then, pulling his head down to hers for a blazing kiss as she came apart. Jack's tongue moved over hers like a wicked promise as he pulled her under him and kneed her thighs apart. The last tremor of her orgasm still vibrated through her as he slid slowly into her, causing the pleasure to continue instead of abate.

She held Jack's intense blue stare as he moved with agonizing slowness, setting a leisurely pace she knew would drive her insane. She bucked and writhed, trying to meet his thrusts, but Jack gripped her hips and kept her steady. Sensation built until she couldn't take it anymore, and she grabbed the headboard as she arched against him and practically screamed his name. Only then did Jack speed up, slamming into her as she clung to him and climaxed again. Vaguely she felt Jack stiffen against her, and heard him shout her name in response.

How long she lay there, waiting for her breathing to even out and her brain to restart, she didn't know. Jack had moved to her side at some point, leaving one heavy thigh draped over hers, and his breath was evening out as well.

Brenna cracked one eye, looked at the clock and groaned. People would be wondering where she was soon if she didn't get moving. And she certainly didn't need Di pounding on her door while Jack was still naked in her bed. She flipped back the sheet and tried to sit up, but Jack's hand on her arm and his leg over hers held her in place.

His eyes were still closed, but he smiled lazily. "Where are you going?"

"To work."

"It's Saturday. Wouldn't you rather stay here? With me?" Jack trailed a hand over her suggestively. Promisingly.

"It's tempting." Her body was primed for a long, lazy morning in bed, but she wiggled out of his grasp before she could give in. "But not all of us are lucky enough to be hotel tycoons. Some of us must go labor in the fields."

One eye opened slightly. "You did that already, remember?"

"And now I must go check the fruits of my labor. Or actually the juice of the fruits." She found her robe on the back of the bathroom door and pulled it on. "Don't you have to go back to the city? Get some work done?"

Jack rolled to his side and propped on his elbow. "I don't *have* to. One of the many perks of being a tycoon, you know, is having people on staff." He crooked a finger at her. "Come here."

Oh, he *was* tempting. His hair stood up in adorable spikes—either from her hands or sleep. Wrapped in a sheet to his waist, with a dark shadow of stubble across his jaw, *this* Jack was one she remembered, and the lure to crawl back into bed was strong.

"Tanks," she muttered.

Jack's eyebrows went up. "You're welcome. I think."

She shook her head at him and went to splash cold

water on her face. *And her libido.* "I said 'tanks'—as in fermentation. I need to go check the temperatures and the sugar levels. I won't be gone long. Maybe a couple of hours."

"Have Ted do it."

"And what excuse would I give him for adding another task to his to-do list today?" Jeans. Bra. Panties. T-shirt. She pulled clothes out of drawers, tossing them onto the bed as she talked.

"You're the boss. You don't have to give reasons."

"Maybe that works at Garrett Properties, but we're a smaller operation here." She bent at the waist to flip her hair over her head as she tackled the mass of tangles. Sex on the floor, sex in the pool, sex in the bed, going to sleep with wet hair—the knots had knots in them.

"I admire your dedication, but seriously, Bren, you have employees for a reason. You don't have to do it all."

"You're one to talk."

"I'm not the one rushing off to work this morning."

From her upside down position, she could see Jack sitting cross-legged on her bed, the sheet tented over his knees. She tugged the comb through one last tangle and stood up straight again, the blood-rush from her head making her wobble a bit as she did so. Jack crooked a finger at her and gave her a look that made her knees wobble for real. At that moment she wanted nothing more than to crawl back under the covers and lose herself in him again.

What was she thinking? Less than twelve hours after

becoming the majority owner of a winery—not to mention the fact she was the vintner as well—and she was already considering shirking her responsibilities because Jack had a magnetism that was near impossible to resist. And what would happen when Jack went back to the city? She'd be left with nothing but a batch of ruined wine.

Jack was temporary. He wasn't for her—she'd learned that the hard way. The sharp stab of regret she felt at that thought only confirmed what she'd admitted yesterday. Jack did still have a piece of her heart. And she was setting herself up for another massive heartbreak.

She must have stood there too long, arguing with herself, because Jack tossed back the covers and crossed the room quickly to catch her hand. He gave a small tug, but she resisted. His eyebrows went up in question.

"What are you doing, Jack?"

That grin of his would be her undoing one day. "Isn't it obvious? Bringing you back to bed."

The fact he was gloriously naked wasn't helping either. But she couldn't let either his grin or his body distract her. "No. I mean what are *we* doing? You and me. Here. Like this."

Jack rolled his eyes. "Do we have to analyze it?"

"Yeah, I think we do." She stepped back and sat on her vanity stool. "I have to admit, my head is still spinning."

"Then why ruin that feeling?"

"Because… Because…" She couldn't find the right words. "All things considered, I think we should quit while we're ahead."

"Meaning?"

Meaning this is a dangerous game I don't want to play. Because I'll lose. "Meaning, I'm glad we've managed to call a ceasefire of sorts, and that we're not sniping at each other anymore. It will make things much easier in the future and last night was great…" She was rambling now, not making a lot of sense, and she knew it. The look Jack was giving her wasn't helping any.

She was making a mess of this, and in another minute or two she'd end up making a fool of herself. She grabbed her clothes and put them on quickly. "Look, um, I really need to get to the winery."

"Brenna…" Jack started.

She backed toward the door, hating the feeling of retreat. *Lord, I'm such a wuss.* But she desperately needed some distance to make sense of this situation and figure out what she was going to say to him. Without babbling next time. "We'll talk later, okay? There's, um, plenty of food and stuff in the fridge. Just make yourself at home. Bye."

Jack called her name as she bolted, the exasperation in his voice very clear even from a distance.

But retreat—no matter how cowardly or graceless— really was the best option right now. Otherwise she was going to make a big fool of herself over him.

Again.

Jack was tempted to go after Brenna, but the scared-rabbit look in her eyes kept him standing still. No need to back her into a corner right now.

He'd been awake less than an hour and his day was

already turning surreal. Brenna certainly had a way of spinning his world off its axis. He'd forgotten what it was like, but oddly enough he didn't feel half as frustrated as he figured he should. Instead, dealing with Brenna seemed to have blown the cobwebs out of his brain, energizing him.

Her retreat this morning—whatever had triggered it—had left his body still burning for her. But now that he wasn't thinking only with his libido, he realized Bren might have a point. The events of the past few days had his head spinning, too, and maybe he should decide what, exactly, his next plan would be.

Amante Verano wouldn't be his problem much longer, but what about Bren?

He really hadn't been awake long enough for his brain to be working properly. He needed coffee. And a shower and a shave.

Then he'd spend some time in Max's office, as he'd originally planned.

That would give Bren time to calm down *and* give him time to decide what he was going to do about her.

She was going to ruin this entire batch of wine, and it would be all Jack's fault. Brenna checked her numbers again, willing them to make sense. It would be nice if *something* made sense today.

In the safety of her office, she'd hoped to find the answers she needed. Three hours later she still didn't have a clear idea of what she wanted, much less what she thought was the right thing to do. The last couple of days with Jack had awakened so many of her old feelings, but new ones were fighting for recognition as well. On the one hand, it seemed as if they were simply picking up where they'd left off, but at the same time it felt different. Like a new start.

But it probably wasn't. This was just an interlude, a hiatus from real life, her mind kept telling her. The idea of starting again, starting over, was just wishful thinking on her part.

Of course none of this was helping her get any work done. For the umpteenth time the scribbles on the paper in front of her swam out of focus and Jack's blue eyes filled her mind. "Damn it." The curse bounced off the fermentation tanks and echoed around the room. This was ridiculous. She glanced over her shoulder, checking the door to the fermentation room was shut firmly, and gave in to her frustration.

Childishly, she flung the notebook to the floor and stomped on it. Then she jumped on it. It didn't help anything, but she felt a tiny bit better after the outburst. She blew her breath out in a huff and picked up the crumpled notebook to smooth out the pages.

"Focus, Brenna, focus," she muttered.

"Am I interrupting something?"

Jack's amused voice spun her around, and she found him leaning against the door and biting back a smile. His hands were in the back pockets of his battered jeans, causing the gray T-shirt he wore to strain over his broad shoulders. From the scuffed work boots to the lock of black hair that fell over his forehead the entire effect was enough to make her heart skip a beat.

This was the Jack she remembered.

She cleared her throat and reached for the pencil stuck through her ponytail. "Just making some notes."

The corner of his mouth quirked up. "With your feet?"

So he'd seen her little temper tantrum. Great. As if it wasn't awkward enough right this second, she also got to add "caught acting like a three-year-old" to her list of cringe-worthy topics of conversation. "It's traditional," she bluffed. "Secret winemaking superstitions handed down through the generations. It's essential to the wine mojo."

Jack nodded sagely. "I see. You don't stomp the grapes anymore, so you stomp the office supplies instead. Interesting."

She straightened her spine. "I don't question *your* business methods…"

His hands came up in appeasement. "Not questioning your methods at all."

She held the notebook close to her chest like a shield, and wrapped her hands tightly around the edges to steady them. "Not to sound, um, rude, but what brings you down here?"

"A sudden interest in deceptively simple Chardonnays?"

There was that smile. The one that usually meant he was thinking about… Her knees wobbled a little, but she gripped the edges of her notebook tighter and forcefully steadied herself. "That isn't Chardonnay."

"Huh? Well, I'm not really—"

"Interested. I know." She sighed, causing Jack to laugh.

"Sorry." He didn't sound the least bit apologetic.

"How about I promise not to tell you what's actually in those tanks, and you promise not to ramble on about stocks or square footage or zoning laws?"

"Deal."

That was easy. Too little, too late, but nice nonetheless. Jack hadn't moved from his casual lean, but her stress level began to increase with his continued presence and increasingly interested look. Why was he here? What was he after? "Jack? Was there something you needed from me?"

"Not really. You said this would only take a couple of hours, and when you didn't come back I came to check everything was okay."

"Sometimes things don't go according to plan. You know how it is." There was an understatement. She didn't even have a plan to deviate from. "Everything okay at the house? Did you find everything you need?"

Jack looked at her oddly. "I got a little bit of work done. I've been going through some of Max's things, and I need to know if there's anything specific you want."

Her heart twinged a little. With everything Jack had stirred up in her recently, she hadn't thought about Max actually being gone in days. "Probably nothing that you want. A couple of photos, Max's sketchbook, the decanter set in the office. Why don't you pack up whatever you want to take, and I'll deal with the rest?"

"All I need is some of Max's paperwork, a few old files."

"Whatever, Jack. Really." Her voice broke a little. It hurt to think of Max's things being divvyed up, but the underlying thought of Jack taking those things *when he left* confirmed her earlier thoughts.

He was beside her in an instant, his face concerned and his hand gentle on her arm. "Are you okay? I'd forgotten this might be tough on you—as close as you and Max were."

Her eyes burned, but she took a deep breath. "How is it not tough for *you*?"

Jack's face clouded briefly. "Max and I had our problems. Our differences. You know that. I'm not saying it doesn't bother me, but I know it's a lot worse for you." He sighed. "I understand, really. If you'd like to wait a while before… There's no real rush, Bren."

"No. It's—it's…" She paused and pulled herself together. "I'm okay. We can do this." Closure all the way around. She patted his hand absently as she spoke, but Jack's hand closed over hers and squeezed. She looked up in surprise.

He was too close. She could count his eyelashes, smell the faint scent of his soap. The concern was still there in his face, but it was tempered by something else. The *something* she'd spent the last hours trying to convince herself wasn't actually there. All the rational pep talks she'd given herself spun away and she felt dizzy.

"Bren…" Jack whispered as he moved another inch closer to her. His fingers twined in hers, and he pulled her hand up to his mouth and traced her knuckles with his lips. "Come back to the house with me."

"I don't think that's a good idea, Jack." Jack's lips snaked across her wrist. Her eyelids felt heavy as they slid shut.

"You're right," he murmured, and her heart sank. This was it. She'd known it was coming. It was for the best.

Then why did it hurt like hell?

He closed the last bit of space, the notebook she still held against her chest the only thing keeping her from being pressed completely against him. She could feel the heavy thud of his heartbeat against her hand. But the words she was bracing herself for didn't come. Instead, his mouth landed on the sensitive skin of her neck.

"What are you doing?"

"Remembering how that sound you make just before you come echoes in this room."

She remembered, too. In blinding detail. The contrast of the cool steel against her back and the hard heat of Jack against her chest and between her legs. Liquid heat pooled in her stomach, and she dropped her notebook in shock. Jack took advantage of both, pressing his body completely against hers and leaning her against the closest tank. Her gasp echoed off the tanks, and she felt his lips curve into a smile at the sound.

Her fingers closed around the soft cotton of his shirt, bracing herself as his free hand slid over the small of her back into the waistband of her jeans. The warmth of his hand after the chill of the tank had her gasping as he pulled her closer still and covered her mouth with his.

The first time Jack had kissed her, they'd been in this room, not far from where they were now. The kiss had left her so dizzy she'd thought something was wrong with the

CO_2 fans. That same feeling swept over her now, as Jack's tongue made a leisurely exploration of her mouth.

A sharp tug at her waist released the snap of her jeans, and a second later Jack's finger dragged a groan from deep in her throat.

A clatter outside reminded her where she was. The huge door to the fermentation room didn't have a lock, and any of her staff could wander in at any moment. She broke the kiss, panting. "Jack. Not here. Someone could—"

Jack kissed her again, cutting off her protest, but then his arm tightened around her waist, lifting her off her feet and maneuvering her behind the largest of the tanks, out of sight of the door.

In the relative privacy they'd found, Jack's kisses became more demanding, his hands more purposeful as clothing was pushed aside, stripped off. Soon she was clinging to him for support, unsure she could handle the onslaught.

Oddly, though, she gained clarity on one thing: the decision she'd been fretting over all morning. The one she'd made but didn't want to admit—not even to herself.

If Jack was going to leave—this time for good—she wanted one last good memory to keep with her. She'd take what he was willing to give.

Would she regret this? Probably. Did she care? Not in the least. For just a little while she wanted to feel like she had when she was eighteen and Jack had wanted her more than anything.

Strong hands closed around her waist, lifting her.

She wrapped her legs around him, and then she couldn't think at all.

She heard her cries of pleasure echoing around her, mixing with the rasping sounds of Jack's breath. She wanted more. Wanted what only Jack could give her.

It wouldn't be enough, but it would have to do.

CHAPTER EIGHT

BRENNA had the most beautiful back. Jack traced his fingers along the indentation of her spine until the sheet draped over her hips stopped his lazy exploration. The sunlight played over her body, bathing her in a golden glow as she lay on her stomach on his bed. Last time he'd checked her eyes had been closed, and their nonsense conversation was easy and relaxed.

But he couldn't keep his hands off her. It was as if his body wanted to make up for lost time—all the years he hadn't had Brenna in his bed.

And suddenly he couldn't remember why that was.

Brenna stretched lazily under his hand and hummed lightly in pleasure. She shifted, turning slightly on her side to face him and resting her head next to his arm. Her fingers traced idly along the arm supporting his body and she sighed deeply in satisfaction.

He pushed her hair over her shoulder to trace the line of her collarbone. "The symphony is hosting a reception Wednesday night, honoring Max's support over the years."

Brenna nodded. "I know. We sent wine."

"But you're not planning to go?"

"Nope."

"Why not?"

She scrunched her nose in displeasure. "The crowds, the small talk—I'm not very good in those situations. You know that."

He did know that. Just another thing they'd fought about more than once. "Still shy in a crowd, huh?"

"I'm not *shy*," Brenna rebutted, "just not good at mingling with people." She shrugged as her fingers moved aimlessly to his chest. "Plus there's the drive down, and since it would be so late I'd have to find a place to stay for the night…"

He laughed. "A place to stay? That's a weak excuse. I own a hotel not four blocks from the concert hall."

Brenna's hand stopped. "Yeah." She narrowed her eyes at him. "And there's that."

Understanding dawned. "Oh. I see. You didn't want to run into me at the party."

"Not to put too fine a point on it, but, yes. I'm avoiding you." She snorted. "Or at least I *was*."

"And now that you're not?"

"Still in the 'not going' camp. There's no one there I really want to see—"

"Except me," he teased.

Brenna pursed her lips and made a face at him. "I know you like these kinds of events, but I don't."

"No one likes these kinds of events. You go because you have to."

"Really?" She pushed up onto her elbow. "You always seemed so keen on them."

"Only in comparison to you and your absolute dread of parties."

Brenna stuck out her tongue and lay back down on her stomach, bunching the pillow under her head.

"You should come, though," he added. When she didn't answer, he pulled out a bigger incentive. "For Max."

"Don't lay a guilt trip on me," she mumbled into the pillow. "The event isn't for Max. It's for Max's money. Max wouldn't care either way."

"True, but as the proprietor of Amante Verano you should be there. You *are* the winery now. It's part of the gig."

She rolled back to face him again, giving him a delicious view. "Ugh. Really?" She looked genuinely displeased at the thought.

"Really." Stroking her stomach lightly, he added, "But you could come with me."

Brenna's eyes widened, and he had to bite back laughter at her horrified yet confused look. "With you?"

"Yes, with me. Do you have a dress?"

"Of course I have a dress." She paused, face crinkling in thought. "Or Di does, at least. But it's still..."

"Come on, Bren. It won't be fun, but it won't suck either."

She flopped back onto the pillow and stared at the ceiling. "Oh, *that's* the way to convince me. I'm not exactly a big symphony fan, you know."

"Then it's a good thing it's not a performance. Simply a meet-and-greet."

Brenna opened her mouth, then closed it and bit her lip. After what looked like an interesting internal conversation, she lifted her head to look at him again. "Are you asking me out? Like on a date?"

He nearly choked, but caught himself and cleared his throat while Brenna stared at him in mild shock. "Well, I am planning to ply you with alcohol and chocolate in an attempt to get you to come back to my place for the evening."

She nodded. "I see. And then?"

The question was casual, but he didn't want any misunderstandings between them. "What are you asking, Bren?"

"I spent years trying to forget about you. And then all the stuff with the winery happens and you're back." She pushed herself to a sitting position. "I find out that not only haven't I forgotten you, I also don't hate you as well. Now we're back here—" she indicated the bed "—and I'm not sure which way to turn."

She wanted an answer, but he didn't have one to give her. "And I don't know what to tell you, Bren. Can't this be enough for now?"

She laughed. "Hell, I'm not sure it's not too much already. Maybe we should just quit while we're ahead. Before things go bad again."

Brenna wasn't wrong about that, but it didn't mean he wanted to take her up on it. "That's the second time today you've played that card."

"Maybe it's worth thinking about."

"Are you kicking me out?"

Her half-smile gave him his answer. "This place is still half yours, you know. For the moment."

He ran a hand down the smooth skin of her arm. "Then I think I'll stay tonight."

"About the symphony thing…"

He lifted a hand to stop her. "I'll send a car. You don't have to get in if you decide you don't want to."

"That sounds fair."

"In the meantime…" He reached for her, and Brenna slid neatly into his arms, molding her body to his. He let her push him onto his back, and the curtain of her hair fell around them, seeming to block out everything else.

This wasn't his average Saturday night. Jack leaned back in his chair at Dianne and Ted's kitchen table and reached for his beer.

With his and Brenna's new truce secure, he'd fully planned to spend the evening in bed, making up for lost time. Around six, though, Brenna had informed him she was due at Dianne's for dinner, and that he was welcome to come along.

He tried to remember what had been on his calendar for tonight—before he'd cleared it to come to Amante Verano. A business dinner? Another charity event? Probably something black-tie.

Instead, he sat at an only partially refinished antique table after a simple family meal, nibbling on cashews and getting soundly beaten in Scrabble.

And, surprisingly, he was enjoying himself.

Brenna held Chloe in her lap, unsuccessfully attempting to keep the tiles out of the baby's reach. "Where's my E?" Brenna asked. "I know I have one.

Aha!" She pried the tile out of Chloe's chubby fist and placed it on the board.

Jack looked at what she played. "Olpe? That's not a word."

Brenna counted her points. "Yes, it is. An olpe is a wine pitcher or flask. Ted?"

Ted nodded. "She's right. It's a word."

Brenna shot him a triumphant look. He countered the look with, "Is it English?"

Dianne returned from the kitchen at that point and leaned against the arm of Ted's chair. "I told you not to play with them. They cheat."

Ted pulled his wife into his lap. "We do not cheat. We just have bigger vocabularies."

Dianne and Ted had been surprised when he'd arrived with Brenna earlier tonight, but after a few interesting looks he didn't quite understand had passed between them and Brenna, they'd set another place at the table for dinner. The conversation had been stilted at first, but they'd warmed up and now treated him like a long-lost family member.

Which, in a way, he guessed he kind of was.

Brenna rescued another tile from Chloe's mouth and handed her a soft toy to play with instead. "There's no need to be a poor loser, Jack."

He looked at the board and at his tiles. Nothing he could play now that Brenna had used the L for her nonexistent word. He shook his head and passed. "I'm wondering why Dianne doesn't get a dictionary and shut you both down."

Her cheeky grin snared him. "Because then it

wouldn't be any fun. Would it, Chloe?" she asked the baby, burying her face in Chloe's neck and making them both giggle.

It was a nice picture. Brenna laughing, relaxed and glowing. Not something he could say he'd seen in a very long time. She was obviously happy, and he was glad he hadn't listened to either his attorneys or his accountants when they'd expressed shock over his plans to give control of the vineyard to Brenna.

"Brenna, I got a call from Charlie today. He says his Chardonnays are almost ready."

That perked Brenna's interest, and she leaned toward Ted. "Wow, that's sooner than expected."

"I'm going to go over tomorrow and test myself, but we could be getting grapes from him early next week."

"Charlie often wants to jump the gun," Brenna cautioned.

"I know, and I'd planned to get ours in first, but…"

Ted and Brenna were just starting to get excited about their conversation when Dianne interrupted. "Stop it, both of you." Dianne rolled her eyes and moved out of Ted's lap. "Can we talk about something else for one night?"

Jack rushed to back her up. "I'm with you, Dianne."

"Thank you, Jack. For once I'm not outnumbered by grape geeks at the table, and I'd like to take advantage of that."

Ted mumbled something under his breath and toyed with his glass. Bren flushed a shade of pink that clashed with her hair. They both looked like children who'd been caught playing with a favorite but off-limits toy.

Ted looked so disappointed Jack almost relented to the conversation.

But it was all he could do not to laugh out loud at them both.

Ted cleared his throat. "Rumor has it a new winery is opening in Napa…"

"Ted!" Dianne chastised.

"What?" Ted spread his hands in innocence. "It's not about *our* wine…"

Brenna caught his eye then, and when he winked at her she smiled in return.

Two hours later Ted carried a sound asleep Chloe to her room as Dianne wished them goodnight and he and Brenna started the walk back to the main house. A full moon lit the vineyard, and crickets chirped all around them. It was quiet otherwise, almost idyllic, and then Brenna slipped her hand into his as they walked. This was more than just a truce—it seemed he and Brenna had something *else* started. And, despite his words earlier, that idea was growing on him a bit.

Brenna squeezed his hand. "You were a good sport tonight."

"Because I let you cheat at Scrabble?"

"I don't cheat." Brenna smacked his arm playfully. "But that's not what I meant. I know tacos and Scrabble aren't your idea of a fun Saturday night, but…"

"I had a good time, Bren."

"Really?"

"Really." Brenna fell quiet and he wondered what she was thinking. "But this is nice, too. I'd forgotten how quiet it gets out here at night."

"It's not San Francisco, that's for sure."

He stopped and pulled her close. "It has its own charms."

Brenna stood on tiptoe to brush a quick kiss across his lips. "It *is* a nice night. Feel like going for a swim?"

A vision of Brenna, wet and slippery, flashed through his mind. He returned the kiss—a hungry one this time, that left Brenna swaying against him—and led her toward the house. "Later."

Brenna's vineyard had one thing San Francisco didn't: Brenna.

CHAPTER NINE

"You know, Brenna, I don't know if this is such a good idea." Dianne carefully unwound a lock of Brenna's hair from around the curling iron and the hot curl landed against Brenna's neck.

Brenna met Di's eyes in the mirror. Dianne shrugged and reached around her for a comb to section off another piece. Brenna sighed. "I know. I mean, me and Jack again? It's crazy and it doesn't make any sense at all, but I just can't help it."

Dianne cleared her throat. "I was actually referring to this up do. I'm not sure your hair will hold the curl."

Brenna flushed. "Oh."

"However," she said, as she twisted and pinned up another lock, "if you'd like to talk about this thing with Jack, I'm certainly willing to listen."

Brenna went back to filing her nails while she thought. Dianne didn't say anything. Finally, unable to meet her eyes again, Brenna asked, "Do you think I'm making a mistake? Getting involved with him again?"

"*Are* you two involved again? I mean, are we talking

about just a little temporary thing or are you thinking this might be long-term?"

Brenna tossed the file onto the vanity. "I wish I knew. This weekend was amazing. After we quit fighting, at least. It's like all the old baggage is gone, and we're kind of starting over." That much was true, and the giddy, light-hearted feeling she remembered so well had her grinning so much most of her employees were giving her strange looks. If only she could shake that other, not-so-giddy feeling that sat low in her chest like a shadow of doom…

"In bed?" Dianne twisted and pinned another piece of hair into place.

"What?" She had to scramble to catch up with the conversation. "Oh. Well, that kinda *is* where we started from the first time."

"And *that* ended well." Dianne snorted.

"We were younger then. This time we're actually talking, too. Ouch! Easy, there."

"Sorry," she muttered. "Hold still, okay?"

Brenna squared her shoulders. "There's a lot to Jack—more than meets the eye—and he seems to understand me now."

"Well, it's good someone does."

She made a face at the mirror. "You're so funny. I'm not that complicated."

"So you say. *I'd* say the fact you're running off to San Francisco to hook up with a guy you couldn't tolerate last week falls smack into the 'beyond-screwed-up' category."

That same thought had occurred to her as well, even if she hadn't wanted to admit it. "So you do think this is a bad idea?"

Di shrugged and reached for the curling iron again. "I don't know what I think. I don't know Jack as well as you do, but I know you don't have a history of making good decisions when it comes to him." Her voice dropped a notch. "I just don't want you to get hurt again."

Me neither, she thought, then shook it off. *People change. Things change.* They could both learn from the past. "I'm an adult. I know what I'm getting into."

"Do you?" Dianne stared sharply at Brenna's reflection. "What's changed? What's so different about *this* time that will keep it from going horribly wrong?"

She'd been asking herself the same question for two days now. "We're older. Wiser. Less volatile. We understand things better now. You saw him Saturday night. Tell me he's not different than he used to be."

"He does seem to be calmer than he used to. And he gets major points for playing along at taco and Scrabble night."

"See? We were just too young to cope with the reality of a relationship. Now we're not."

"That's great, Brenna. Really." Di's words sounded forced.

"You think I should quit while I'm ahead?"

Dianne rested her hands on Brenna's shoulders and squeezed gently. "I just want you to be happy, Brenna. If Jack can do that, then great—I'm on board. But don't let one fabulous weekend in bed and those flowers blind you to everything else. Use your head this time, too, okay?"

Brenna thought of the enormous arrangement of peonies and hydrangea on her desk in the office.

"How'd you know about my flowers?" The flowers had arrived Monday afternoon, but Brenna had intercepted the delivery up by the entrance to the vineyard. No one had seen them arrive—or at least that was what she'd thought—and she'd stashed them where no one— Dianne specifically—should have seen them. At least Di didn't know about the late-night phone calls…

"That's what you pay me for, right?" Dianne pushed one more pin into the mass of Brenna's hair and eyed it critically. "That should do it. Close your eyes."

Brenna did, and Dianne sprayed her handiwork liberally with hairspray. Coughing, Brenna waved the mist away from her face.

"What do you think?" Di asked.

Long, loose ringlets framed her face, while the rest of her hair was up in an artfully arranged chignon. "You're a genius, Di. Now for the dress…"

Brenna held her breath as Dianne worked the zipper. The simple black sheath hugged her curves, making her feel feminine and elegant, and the beading around the neck and hem caught the light of the afternoon sun and sparkled. She slid her feet into Dianne's prized pair of slingbacks, and twirled in front of the mirror. "Wow," she said to her reflection.

Dianne eyed her critically and tugged at the hem of the dress, straightening it. "Wow is right. You clean up nicely, Brenna."

"In your clothes." She laughed as Dianne handed her jewelry and a handbag. "I'd be going to this shindig in jeans if not for you."

"That's my lucky dress. It's what I was wearing the

night I met Ted." Di collapsed into the chair Brenna had only recently occupied and smiled at the memory.

Brenna winked at her. "Sounds more like a get lucky dress. All the better."

"You don't need my dress to get lucky tonight. Just be careful, okay?"

"Your dress is safe. I doubt Jack will be ripping it off my body."

Dianne stared at her evenly. "I'm not worried about the dress."

A movement of something black outside her window caught Brenna's attention, and she moved the curtains fully aside to check. "Jack sent a limo. He doesn't do anything halfway, does he?" She grabbed her overnight bag and shawl.

"Brenna…"

"I hear you, Di. And I will be careful. I'm not some naïve kid anymore." She wrapped Dianne in a one-armed hug. "Thank you. For everything."

"Have fun. You'll be home when? Tomorrow? Friday?"

"I'll be back by Friday for sure. Jack leaves for New York that morning. Hold down the fort for me."

"I will."

"Just don't forget to check—"

"It's under control. Go. Have fun."

She didn't recognize the chauffeur who took her bags and offered a hand to help her in the car, but he had a friendly smile as he introduced himself as Michael.

"And may I say how lovely you look, Miss Walsh?"

"Thank you." She settled back against the butter-soft seats and sighed. The last time she'd been in a limo Jack had been with her. They'd been out somewhere, but left early because they were fighting again. They'd reconciled in the privacy of the back seat, and she'd knocked the decanter of Scotch to the floor with her enthusiasm. They'd been drunk off the fumes by the time they'd arrived home…

That was the story of her life with Jack. Fight. Make up. Fight. Make up. The when, the where and the what might change, but the pattern was part of the whole. Funny how she couldn't quite remember what that fight had been about, but she could remember exactly how Jack had held her, and the things he'd whispered in her ear…

Man, it was stuffy in here. She fumbled with the air vent, directing the cool air at her heated cheeks. Di's concerned face swam into focus. She had a point: why should this time be any different? And what, exactly, was she hoping for? A new start with Jack? Just a good time? And for how long?

Miles of vineyards flew past her window in a blur as the limo passed through the Sonoma Valley toward the city. Much more than fifty miles separated Amante Verano from San Francisco. It was a whole different world—one that she'd failed miserably to join or even enjoy the last time.

Was Dianne right? Was she walking right back into a disaster? Had this weekend been just Jack humoring her, or could he really want her—Scrabble and all—again?

It *could* be different, she told herself. She and Jack

didn't have any misconceptions about each other any-more. They knew where they stood, and she was a big enough girl to know when to pull the plug on this ex-periment. But she'd never forgive herself if she didn't at least *try*. She'd always wonder otherwise…

Belatedly, she noticed the small bouquet of flowers tucked into a vase on the bar. White orchids tied with a red ribbon, with a small envelope peeking out of the blooms. As she pulled it free she saw her name written across the front in Jack's bold handwriting. It felt lumpy in her hand as she released the flap and pulled out the note inside.

Glad you decided to come after all. See you soon.

Jack's initials, MJG, were scrawled in the corner, almost illegible if she hadn't seen them a million times before. She shook the envelope and something sparkly landed in her hand.

A bracelet. No, an anklet. The sunlight, muted slightly through the tinted windows, caused the rubies set in a thin gold chain to flash. Rubies—because she'd told him once that diamonds were too cold and rubies reminded her of her wines.

Jack had a good memory. Orchids and peonies, not roses. Rubies, not diamonds. An anklet because she didn't like bracelets because they caught on things. Little things that should have faded from his memory long ago, but touched her now simply because they hadn't.

She propped her foot on the seat and fastened the chain around her ankle. The slowing of the car caused her to look up, and she saw the orange railings of the

Golden Gate Bridge. How had she got here so fast? This really was the point of no return.

The limo crawled through the city traffic at an infuriating pace. Now that she'd made the decision, got in the car and clasped Jack's gift around her ankle, she was eager to see him. Her heartbeat picked up as the limo pulled to a stop. But it wasn't the multi-colored awning of Garrett Towers outside her window.

It was the concert hall.

Michael opened her door and extended a hand to her. "Don't we need to go get Jack first?" She didn't want to imply Michael had forgotten to stop at Garrett Towers...

"No, Miss Walsh, Mr. Garrett asked me to bring you directly here."

"So he's inside?"

"Mr. Garrett has been delayed in a meeting. He will meet you here shortly." Michael extended his hand again to help her out.

She definitely didn't want to go inside alone. "Can't you take me back...?" She stopped as Michael's eyebrows went up a fraction of an inch. Of course not. That would be silly.

She was an adult; she could walk into a party by herself. More importantly, she was the owner of Amante Verano, Max's pride and joy, and this party was in his honor. She allowed Michael to help her from the limo, and took a deep breath to steady herself as a doorman opened the massive entry doors for her.

She could do this. No problem.

She was also going to kill Jack Garrett later.

* * *

An hour later, Brenna was plotting inventive and painful ways for Jack to die as she made awkward small talk with strangers. The fake smile was starting to hurt her cheeks, and she wished she'd stuck to her earlier resolution not to come at all.

Everyone had known Max, so he was a safe and easy topic of conversation for her, but without fail the conversation would turn quickly to Max's other interests in San Francisco—which she knew little to nothing about—and then on to people she didn't know and places she'd never been. She had nothing to add to the conversation, and she could only ask so many questions before she began to look like some hayseed hick from the boonies.

She certainly felt like one.

A server offered her another glass of wine, and for the first time in her life she declined. The caterers had the Cabernet too cold and the Chardonnay too warm, totally ruining them both. But several people, on learning she was the vintner at Amante Verano, complimented her on the wines. One older gentleman, who owned a chain of popular restaurants across the state, seemed very interested in adding her wines to his wine list. Jack had been right about that much: this was as much a business affair as a social one. She didn't feel bad, since it was Max's celebration anyway and he'd be happy to see his wines' reputation grow, but if she was making business contacts here it meant everyone else was, too, and that just felt wrong.

Escaping to the ladies' room, she touched up her lipstick and checked to see Di's up do was staying put.

For once, Di was wrong: her hair was holding the curls just fine, and none had escaped the mass of pins she'd used to hold them in place.

She stared at herself in the mirror, oddly pleased with herself. In spite of everything, she'd handled this event just fine. A small smile tugged at the corner of her mouth: she, of all people, had just mingled her way into what could lead to a lucrative business contact. A small surge of pride moved through her.

She hesitated, though, before heading back out into the party proper, and glanced at her watch one last time.

Jack was now an hour and a half late. *Damn it.* What was keeping him?

"Excuse me. Have we met?"

Brenna turned to see a woman about her age; while her face looked vaguely familiar, she couldn't place her. She plastered a smile on her face regardless. "Possibly. I'm Brenna Walsh, from Amante Verano Cellars." At the woman's blank look, she added helpfully, "Max Garrett's vineyard?"

"Oh, you're Jack's ex."

She'd known this moment would come. "Yes, that, too."

"Is Jack here?"

"Not yet, but he is planning to come."

"Oh, good. It's been ages since I've seen him." The woman opened her purse and pulled out a lipstick.

"And you are…?" Brenna prompted.

"Libby Winston. We met years ago at another event. I think it was shortly after you and Jack got married."

Brenna still couldn't place her, and it must have shown on her face.

"You probably met so many of Jack's friends, and it was so long ago…"

Embarrassed, she tried to explain. "I'm terribly sorry. I'm really bad at…"

Libby brushed the apology away. "Don't worry about it. You were so shy and quiet. I'm not surprised you don't remember many of Jack's friends." Libby smiled, but it held no warmth at all. "Everyone remembers you, of course. Jack really surprised us all, getting married like that. And we certainly weren't expecting *you*, either."

What was that supposed to mean? She tried to sound flippant. "That's the thing about whirlwind romances. They surprise everyone."

"Thank goodness you came to your senses, then. I never could figure out what brought you two together."

Brenna officially no longer liked Libby Winston.

Libby's eyes narrowed in curiosity. "You and Jack aren't back together again, are you?"

Brenna nearly choked. She had a feeling Libby might be overly interested in the answer, and after Libby's earlier comment she was tempted to say yes. But Brenna herself wasn't even completely sure *what* she and Jack were right now. "Jack and I are business partners." It wasn't a complete lie. Technically, they still were. She hadn't signed the sale agreement yet.

"That must be interesting, considering your past."

"Actually, it's working out quite well." Thankfully her phone beeped, alerting her to an incoming text message. Jack. About damn time. "Excuse me. I need to take care of this."

She slipped out the door before Libby could bring up any other uncomfortable subjects and read Jack's message: *"By the bar. Where are you?"*

A quick glance toward the bar, and she spotted his dark head scanning the crowd. When he spotted her, she waved, and his answering smile gave her a jolt even through her ire at his tardiness.

"Bren, you look incredible."

He leaned in to kiss her gently on the cheek and she muttered through her teeth, "You're late."

"Unavoidable," he whispered.

"You're dead meat."

"I'll make it up to you." He pulled back, still wearing that same smile for anyone watching. Stepping back, he let his eyes roam appreciatively down her body. "You look better than incredible."

The look sent a zing of electricity through her. Damn it, he wasn't getting off that easy. He'd asked her to come, and she had. The least he could have done was *be* here. "Flattery will get you nowhere."

Tugging on her hand, he pulled her close again and said quietly, "Then let me start making it up to you now."

"What? How?" Jack was leading her behind the crowd, out a side door by the kitchen, and down a back hallway as she sputtered her questions. "Where are you taking me?"

In answer, he pushed open a door marked "Private. Rehearsal Room One." The door closed behind them, and she heard the lock snap into place. "I apologize for being late. There was a problem with the New York property I had to sort out."

"And you had to bring me here to apologize?" The small room held a baby grand piano and a music stand, but little else.

"No, I brought you here because I've missed you." Jack sat on the piano bench and pulled her into his lap. "And this room is soundproof."

That was all the warning she got before his mouth landed on hers.

CHAPTER TEN

INDICATING the man to his right, Jack said, "Brenna, I'd like to introduce you to the Mayor."

Brenna's knees were still weak from their frenzied trip to the rehearsal room, and she knew her cheeks were still flushed. Meeting the Mayor, the Artistic Director, and the First Violin ten minutes after a mind-blowing orgasm…surreal. She might not have forgiven Jack completely for being over an hour late, but she was less upset about it now, at least. It still bothered her to think where she ranked on his priority list, but he had searched her out immediately once he did arrive.

And pulled her away for a quickie. As the afterglow faded and Jack glad-handed his way around the room—leaving her alone again quite a bit—her view on that experience began to change a little, too. She felt like a convenience—or an inconvenience, depending how she looked at it.

But standing at Jack's side while he mingled wasn't much better either. She got to talk to the same people she'd met earlier. Or at least she got to listen to them. If the conversation had been difficult earlier, it was worse now. The hayseed hick feeling came back in full force, because Jack *did* know all the people and *had* been to all the places. And she still had nothing to add to the conversation.

Two and a half hours down. She might make it through the last thirty minutes, but her patience was wearing thin. She kept the smile on her face, though. After all, these were Jack's friends and associates. She owed him a sincere attempt after he'd done so well with *her* friends.

More people had connected the mental dots now, and she received several curious stares as folks tried to figure out why Jack was here with his ex-wife. The more forthright just asked directly. While she tried to explain her connection to Max through Amante Verano, it rarely satisfied anyone. If one more person referred to her as "Jack's ex," she'd pull her own hair out. And Jack wasn't exactly correcting them either. Not that she necessarily *wanted* to spread the word prematurely that she and Jack were seeing each other again, but she figured that trip to the rehearsal room at least took her out of the "ex" category.

"Jack! You're finally here." Libby Winston leaned in a little too close as she greeted Jack with air kisses. Wrapping her manicured hand around Jack's arm, Libby anchored herself to his side. If Jack minded the obvious fawning, he certainly didn't put a stop to it, and it made Brenna a bit nauseous to watch.

"Libby, you remember Brenna?"

"Of course. Brenna and I actually ran into each other earlier in the Ladies'. You two have certainly got speculation flying, being here together like this." Libby batted her eyelashes at Jack insipidly.

Oh, please. That had to be the most unsubtle attempt to pry out information she'd ever heard.

"Brenna is running Max's winery now," Jack answered smoothly.

"She said you two were business partners?"

I'm standing right here, you know. Of course it wasn't the first time she'd felt invisible tonight, but coming from Libby it was really grating her nerves.

Jack inclined his head, acknowledging the statement without further response, and Brenna wanted to smack him.

Libby forged ahead. "We missed you at Harry and Susan's Saturday night."

"I spent the weekend at the vineyard."

Libby's eyebrows moved the millimeter allowed by botox. "*You*, Jack? Rusticating in wine country? The wonders never cease."

How much longer would she have to stand here and listen to this?

"There's a first time for everything." Jack flashed Libby his ladykiller smile, and Libby practically swooned.

"I trust it won't be a regular occurrence, then? Weekends in the country?"

"Surely you know me better than that, Libby?"

Libby narrowed her eyes at Brenna, but Brenna held the same smile she'd worn all evening. She wouldn't give Libby the satisfaction. She, better than anyone, knew Jack's feelings about wine country.

Libby batted her eyelashes at Jack again before

turning to Brenna. "I promised Tom and Margaret I'd round Jack up—" Libby paused and blinked. "Do you know Tom and Margaret, Brenna?"

Of course she didn't, and she'd bet next season's Chardonnay Libby knew that. "Can't say I've had the pleasure."

"That's a shame. But," she continued, "I *did* promise them I'd drag Jack over so they can finalize those plans for the golf tournament. Do you mind, Brenna?"

"Not at all." *Twenty more minutes. That's it.*

"Bren, would you...?" Jack started, but she waved him silent.

"Actually, I think I'll just get a refill while you all talk business."

Jack looked at her strangely. "I'll only be a minute."

"No problem."

Libby dragged Jack away before the words were fully out of her mouth. Jack didn't even play golf. Or did he? He might have picked up the hobby sometime in the last decade.

Draining the last of her soda, she handed the empty glass to a passing waiter and went to find a place to sit. She slid her feet out of Dianne's shoes and wiggled her toes in relief. The feeling didn't extend to her mind, though.

Brenna felt as if she was having a flashback to their marriage. Hell, the whole damn night felt like a re-run. The awkward conversations with his friends, being an outsider... They'd go home, fight, and have make-up sex. But the next outing would bring more of the same. She snorted. They'd already *had* the fight and the make-up sex tonight. The cycle was complete. History repeated itself. She'd given it her best shot and still fallen short.

A high-pitched laugh caught her attention over the music, and she looked over to see Libby Winston's head thrown back in over-dramatic style as she found whatever Jack was saying to be hilarious. Libby swatted Jack's arm playfully, then pulled him close to whisper something in his ear. Jack wore a look of mild amusement as Libby practically shoved her breasts in his face.

It was sickening to watch.

She knew she shouldn't care, but she couldn't help the feeling coiling in her stomach. Even more, she didn't like what that might mean for her.

She shouldn't have come tonight. She'd been right in her first decision not to come, but for all the wrong reasons. She could be the face of Amante Verano, shake hands and network just fine. It was everything else that was horribly wrong.

But the trip wasn't in vain. She'd made some good business connections. Hell, she'd even met the Mayor. But this event had also brought home the truth she'd been fighting against all along.

At least she'd been reminded *before* she got in too deep this time. She and Jack were from different worlds—Libby Winston had just driven that point home for her—and getting involved with him again wouldn't end any better this time.

Something was bothering Brenna. On the surface she seemed fine, smiling and chatting with some of the biggest names in the community. He'd had many compliments on the wine, and he hoped Brenna was taking advantage of the opportunity to network.

Even though she smiled and nodded and charmed who she could, he could tell something wasn't right. Tension hummed under everything she said to him, and he could see the uncomfortable set to her shoulders. Even her smile had lost its sparkle.

She slid into the limo with an audible sigh of relief. "Thank God that's over."

Why was she sitting on the opposite seat? "You did great."

"That doesn't mean it wasn't horrible."

"Well, it's over now, and the night can only get better from here, right?"

"I wouldn't count on that." Brenna reached for one of the decanters, sniffed the contents, then poured herself a glass. The tension he'd sensed earlier must have been repressed hostility, because it now filled the air around them.

"Are you still mad because I was late?"

Crossing her arms across her chest, she shot him a dirty look. "It's certainly a place to start."

"I told you, it was unavoidable."

She rolled her eyes. "It always is with you. You *wanted* me to come to this party, and then you couldn't be bothered to even show up on time."

He sighed. "How many times do I have to apologize for that?"

"Don't bother. We've had *that* fight before. I know how it ends."

Exasperation set in. Brenna wasn't making sense. "Then what?"

That lit her fire, and the look she leveled on him nearly scorched him. "I don't even know where to begin. The wham-bam-thank-you-ma'am in the rehearsal room?"

Wham-bam...? What the hell...?

"Or the fact that right after that I got to watch you flirt with half the female population of San Francisco?"

That was what had her upset? "I was simply being nice."

She snorted, and turned to stare pointedly out the window.

"Are you jealous, Bren?" He couldn't keep the amazed amusement out of his voice.

That snapped Brenna's eyes back to his. "No. Not in the least. I just think it's rude to expect me to stand there and watch you eat up all that simpering."

"So you'd rather I be rude to them?"

"Polite party conversation doesn't require your head in Libby's cleavage. And it certainly—" She choked on her ire and turned back to the window. "You could've put a stop to it, but you didn't. It's like I wasn't even there."

The twelve blocks back to Garrett Towers took only a few minutes at this time of night, and they were already pulling to a stop under the awning. The night doorman had the door open seconds later, and Brenna was out of the limo before Jack could even respond to her last comment.

But her game face was back in place as she smiled at the doorman and they walked calmly to the elevator.

Brenna's jealousy was a new experience for him, and, while he didn't look forward to trying to talk her out of her anger, the fact she was jealous at all did bring him a small bit of satisfaction.

Once the elevator doors closed, he tried to talk her down. "I would think that trip to the rehearsal room proved you have no reason at all to be jealous. In fact, I'm willing to spend all night proving it to you."

"Not a chance," she scoffed. "I'm just going up long enough to get my suitcase. I'm going home."

"Home?" he repeated dumbly. "Now?"

"Yes, now." She shot him a level look as the elevator doors opened. "You don't even have to order a car for me this time. I can do it myself."

The chauffeur had left Brenna's bag sitting right inside the door, and she grabbed the handle, obviously intending to get right back on the elevator. He stopped her by closing the door and standing in front of it. With all he knew now, he wasn't going to let Brenna retreat again. "Are you really going to storm out of here just because you're jealous of Libby and her posse?"

"I'm going home because I realized tonight that I was crazy to think anything would be different this time. Libby Winston's swooning is only part of it. I won't just be your accessory again."

Ah, finally they were at the heart of the matter. Unfortunately, he wasn't quite sure what that was. He approached her carefully. "Again?"

"Jack…" Brenna's jaw clenched.

"Spit it out, Bren. If you're not just jealous of Libby, then what is the problem?"

Brenna dropped the handle of her suitcase. That was good news. At least he'd kept her from running out on him.

She crossed her arms and cocked an eyebrow at him. "The problem is you."

"Me?"

"Yes, you. You want a list?"

The gauntlet was down now; he couldn't wait to hear this. "Please. No need to hold back."

"Fine." Brenna stomped across the room and sank gracefully onto the couch, her spine ramrod-straight with anger. Her voice dripped with icy, sarcastic politeness as she started on her litany. "We'll skip over the lateness, since that's just par for the course."

Personally, he felt that statement deserved addressing, but Brenna moved on before he could.

"We'll also skip past the fact you let everyone dismiss me as just your ex, since technically I am. The five minutes in the rehearsal room notwithstanding, of course."

He nearly choked at the insult. Five minutes? It had been closer to twenty really good, intense minutes, and he was tempted to remind her how she hadn't been complaining at the time, but he bit his tongue for the moment.

"Half the time you treated me like I wasn't even there. And you let everyone else do it, too. Just because I don't travel in the same circles and I don't know the same people, that doesn't mean I'm invisible."

He was damned no matter what he tried to do. "I know you don't like these kinds of events, and after leaving you on your own for so long I thought you'd *like* not having to be on the spot for the rest of the evening."

Her eyes narrowed. "You thought I couldn't handle it? After I'd been handling it for the last hour just fine? Why the hell did you want me to come in the first place?"

Brenna wasn't known for her reasonableness when she was angry, but now they were going in circles. He tried to keep his frustration in check. "I know you can handle it, Bren, I just thought you didn't *want* to."

"And you didn't see how we'd time-warped back ten years?"

Brenna was getting more worked up instead of calming down. This was *not* his plan for tonight.

Brenna shook her head when he didn't respond. "Hell, you and Libby seemed to forget I was even standing there."

Back to Libby. So Brenna *was* jealous. Not that her other complaints weren't valid, and they probably did deserve addressing at a later time, but Brenna's jealousy—obvious now, even though she tried to hide it—was definitely more interesting and pertinent to the matter at hand.

"Libby Winston might be a terrible flirt," he said as he crossed the space between them and joined her on the couch.

"In many ways," Brenna muttered.

He bit back a smile. "But she's no threat to you."

Jack's sincerity shook her. As did his proximity. The tension simmering between them had moved from hostility to something more, and taken on a sharper edge. This was exactly why the make-up sex was always so intense. One type of heat led to another. Even now.

"I am *not* threatened by Libby and her surgically enhanced self," she countered, but even she could hear the outright bluff in her voice and she hated it. She scooted back a little, trying to put distance between the meaningful glow in Jack's eyes and her already weakening resolve.

She didn't want to be jealous of Libby Winston. She didn't like what that implied about her and her inability to fit into that part of Jack's life. Again.

And she definitely didn't want Jack's assurances that he wanted her, not Libby, to affect her the way they did.

It meant she was already too far in. She was going to get hurt, and neither her heart nor her ego could take that punch. While part of her wanted to end this right now, to take her pride while she still had it and head back to the safety of Amante Verano, she couldn't seem to gather the energy to get off the couch.

"Bren…" Jack's hand was on her knee, his fingers tracing a small circle and causing goosebumps to rise all over her body. Damn him. No, damn *herself*. She was mad at him. Really mad, yet her body had already forgotten everything else, and her blood was beginning to surge through her veins in anticipation.

"Jack…" She tried to protest.

"If I'd known you didn't mind the whole of San Francisco knowing exactly how we spent the weekend, I would have gladly corrected anyone who tried to categorize you as simply my ex."

His hand moved higher, distracting her from his words. She forced herself to concentrate.

"And if Libby Winston or anyone else in that room

was even the smallest bit deserving of your jealousy I wouldn't have needed to coerce you to come tonight— or dragged you off to the rehearsal room."

There went the rest of her anger, smothered by the seductive promise in his voice. Breathing became difficult as he leaned closer.

"Do you doubt me, Bren?"

God, the man oozed pure sex appeal out of every pore. Even as he calmed her with his words, she could feel the desire he was holding carefully—if temporarily—in check vibrating in the air.

"I don't doubt that you want me. But I—I…" She couldn't quite get the words out. Clearing her throat, she made her stand. "That's not enough this time. I want more than that."

A look she hadn't seen in years crossed his face. She'd almost forgotten it, but she recognized it the moment it appeared. And her heart skipped a beat at the sight. There. *That* was her Jack. A small smile tugged at the corner of his mouth. "More, huh?"

"More."

He tugged slightly on her hand, and she slid across the leather until they were only inches apart. "More sounds like an interesting idea."

Jack's hand trailed up her arm to smooth across the curve of her shoulder before it moved to her back. *Focus.* "I don't know if we're capable of that. We always end up fighting. Just like tonight." Her voice trembled a little as her body fell into habit: they'd fought, and now it was time to make up. Her muscles loosened and her pulse kicked up in anticipation.

"Some things are important enough to fight for. And you're worth fighting with." The husky undertone affected her almost as much as the words. She felt the zip of Dianne's lucky dress give way as he eased it down.

She was a goner and she knew it. She couldn't fight it any longer, and she didn't want to either. God help her, she was still in love with Jack.

CHAPTER ELEVEN

HER phone was ringing.

The chirpy noise filtered into her dream and pulled her to semi-consciousness. No light filtered through her eyelids, so it had to be very late. Or maybe very early.

Jack's arm had her pinned to the bed. His body curved around hers, and her feet were tangled in the sheets. Getting out of bed wasn't tempting at all—much less for what was probably a wrong number anyway.

The noise stopped, and Brenna let sleep start to tug her back under. She was exhausted, thanks to Jack. Make-up sex had never been like that. Although neither one of them had said anything outright, the dynamic had shifted somehow, and they'd have to address that eventually.

She was looking forward to it.

When the chirping started again, she sighed. Even Jack stirred this time.

"Is that your phone?" he mumbled.

"Yes. It's probably just a wrong number."

"Then you're not going to answer it?"

"No."

"Good." Jack pulled her closer and adjusted his hold

on her, snuggling her in against his chest. His deep sigh of satisfaction seemed to slide through her, warming her soul. She could feel the smile on her face as she closed her eyes and—

Jack's phone blared like a Klaxon, jarring them both wide awake. As Jack cursed under his breath and pushed to a sitting position alarm bells started clanging in her head. The chances of both of them getting wrong number calls so close together... Something wasn't right.

Jack retrieved his pants from the floor and fished in the pocket for his phone, while Brenna made her way to the other room to find her purse. She pulled out her phone and flipped it open. She could hear Jack's voice as he answered, but couldn't make out any of the words as she scrolled through the menu on her phone. Two missed calls from Amante Verano's main line. Her heart stopped beating.

She didn't seem to have any voicemail waiting, but deep down she knew Jack was getting whatever news there was right now. She should go in, eavesdrop on Jack's side of the conversation and see what she could figure out, but something held her back. It couldn't be good news. Not at this time of night.

Then Jack appeared in the doorway, his phone still in his hand. The look of concern and pity on his face confirmed her earlier thought: the news—whatever it was—wasn't good. Her knees shook a little.

He seemed to be searching for words. "That was Ted."

Oh, God. "Was someone hurt? Di? Was there an accident?"

"No one was hurt. Everyone is fine," he reassured her, and the relief that washed over her staggered her. But the relief was painfully short-lived; she could tell the worst was yet to come.

"*What*, Jack. Tell me."

He took a deep breath. "There was a fire."

"*Fire?*" Of all the possibilities... "Oh, my God. Where? When?" She was already in the bedroom, searching through her suitcase, pulling out clothes and trying to dress with shaking hands.

Jack caught her arms and held her—forcing her to look at him directly, yet still offering his support. "In the winery itself. Bren..." He blew out his breath in a long, noisy sigh. She braced herself. "The building is a total loss."

"Tot—" She couldn't get the word past the lump in her throat. "Oh, God."

"I'm so sorry, Bren."

Total. She couldn't process it. Her winery was gone? "I need to...need to..." She looked at the clothes in her hand and had no idea what to do with them.

"Finish getting dressed. We'll leave whenever you're ready."

She'd never been so tired in her life, but there was no way she could sleep. There was too much to do, and while her brain spun at top speed, she couldn't shake the weight that kept her moving sluggishly and mechanically.

They'd arrived at Amante Verano at sunrise, but the beautiful picture that normally greeted her had been scarred by the charred, blackened ruins of the winery.

Everything else looked the same as it had when she'd left yesterday—*God, had it really been less than twenty-four hours?*—and the surreal disconnect only added to the problems she was having making her thoughts fall into logical order.

Jack had been there for her, holding her hand while Ted filled her in on the details. When it came to what needed to be done next—calling the insurance company, talking to the Fire Marshal—he'd taken over, with her blessing and heartfelt thanks.

In fact, Jack was in her office right now—where she should be, *would* be as soon as she could muster the strength to stand. Instead, she sat cross-legged on the ground, unable to stop staring at what was left of her winery. The walls leaned at drunken angles, barely holding up what was left of the roof. The giant hole in the side wall—caused when the tank full of neutral grape spirits exploded, Ted said—mirrored the feeling in her stomach.

She needed to quit wallowing. Ted was burning up the phone lines, trying to find someone to take the grapes off their hands. They still needed to harvest next week, or else lose the crop entirely, but they needed somewhere to send those grapes once they did. She should be helping with that chore, or doing any of the dozen other things waiting for her, and she would.

In just another minute.

If Max were alive, Jack would gladly read him the riot act over the astounding lack of proper insurance this place had. This was a giant mess. Max had certainly known the implications of underinsuring, so Jack could only assume Max had figured he'd play the odds and use his own money should those odds ever not work out in his favor. It looked as if Brenna also knew the winery was underinsured, and had planned to remedy that, but for whatever reason hadn't done so yet. The road to recovery would be rough, to say the least. Without a serious infusion of cash, Amante Verano might not recover at all.

And he had a feeling Brenna understood that on some level.

He hadn't seen much of Brenna since shortly after they'd arrived. In a sort of unspoken agreement Brenna had taken charge of the "wine side"—conferring with Ted and Dianne on grapes and stock issues—while he had done what he did best and buried himself in paperwork and crunched numbers as night fell.

In the wake of that thought he heard footsteps in the hall, and Brenna entered the office. She'd been pale and haunted-looking in the car on the way out this morning, and the events of the day hadn't helped her any. For lack of a better word, Brenna looked fragile—a sharp contrast to her normal energy and strength—and dark circles shadowed her eyes.

"How's it look?" she asked as she collapsed into her chair opposite Max's desk.

"Honestly, Bren, it's not great." He wanted to cushion the blow if he could. "There are options, but…"

"But they're not great. I figured as much." She sighed, and scrubbed her hands over her face.

He noticed the soot on her hands. He should have

known Brenna wouldn't be able to stay away from the building entirely, as the Fire Marshal had recommended. "How are you holding up?"

She laughed bitterly. "Not great. Ted's having a little luck finding buyers for some of the fruit." She sighed. "Box wine. My grapes are going to be made into cheap box wine. My mother is rolling in her grave."

"You're doing the best you can under the circumstances, Bren."

"I know. It doesn't lessen the feeling, though." Another deep sigh, and Brenna shook her head as if to clear it. "Any other news I need to know about? What did the Fire Marshal say?"

"Other than 'Stay away from the building,' you mean?" Brenna dropped her eyes. "It's all preliminary, but he thinks he knows what started the fire."

That got Brenna's attention. "Really? Already?"

"Yeah. It was electrical in nature; that much he's pretty sure of. It looks like a short in the main pump sparked it."

He didn't think it could be possible, but Brenna went even paler behind her freckles as she pulled in her breath sharply. "The pump?" she whispered.

She looked as if she was about to pass out. He came out from behind the desk and squatted in front of her as she took deep breaths. "Are you all right, Bren?"

"Oh, my God. This is *my* fault."

"How could it possibly be your fault?"

Brenna stood and wrapped her arms around her stomach. "The pump's been acting up lately. I took it apart last week. Twice, actually." When she looked at him, the horror in her eyes shocked him. "This is my fault. *I* burned down my winery."

"It's not your fault. The findings are still preliminary, and they could change." She started to protest, but in her current state he needed to talk her down. "Even if it was the pump, it's still not your fault. I know you, Bren, and you could take that thing apart in your sleep. You didn't cause this."

She didn't seem comforted. If anything, she became more agitated. "Half a dozen owners, Prohibition, droughts, phylloxera—no problem. My family has produced the best fruit and the best wine in the valley regardless of the circumstances. But *I* take over, and I destroy everything in a month because I can't put a stupid pump back together properly."

"Bren…" He reached for her, but she flinched away from his hand.

"Don't!" Her voice shook as she took two steps back. In a slightly calmer, although still shaking voice, she whispered, "Please don't touch me. I can't handle it. I'm barely holding myself together as it is."

All the more reason to give her someone to hold on to, as far as he figured, but Brenna was already out of reach. "You look exhausted. Why don't you go rest for a little while? Or we could get something to eat if you want. Later we'll sit down and come up with a plan."

She swallowed hard. "You're right. I could use a break. I think I will go lie down. I'll see you later." She walked from the room, still muttering to herself. *Probably still beating herself up over that damn pump.*

A ping from the computer brought him back to the other business clamoring for his attention. He couldn't leave Brenna and the vineyard right now, so he'd emailed Roger earlier and informed him of the change of plans. He couldn't postpone the meetings in New York on such short notice, so Roger would have to go in his place. Unfortunately, bringing him up to speed was taking a bit more time than he'd hoped.

After an hour of back and forth emails and a phone call he finally had it sorted out. Brenna hadn't reappeared, and all seemed quiet, so he went to the kitchen for a beer.

A moment later Brenna stuck her head around the door. Her color was a bit better now, but she still wore that tired, haunted look. Her hair hung in a slightly damp curtain around her face. Obviously fresh from a shower, she wore a baggy T-shirt and pajama pants. Red toenails peeked out from under the floppy hems.

She cleared her throat. "I'm sorry about earlier. I shouldn't have snapped at you like that."

"It's understandable."

"Thanks. It's not been a good day. I feel like I've come loose from my trellis and I'm just flapping in the breeze."

"You'll get through this. It may sound trite, but it's true."

"The thing is…" She paused and took another of those deep breaths. "It really means a lot to me that you're here. You didn't have to come—"

"Of course I did."

She shook her head. "Actually, you didn't. And I overheard you talking on the phone earlier. I know you've canceled your trip to New York so you can stay here during all this. I really appreciate it."

Her hands pleated the hem of her T-shirt, telling him she had something more to say. "You know, I've been feeling kind of lonely out here, and when I saw the—" Her voice cracked. She swallowed and tried again. "When I saw what was left, I thought I'd hit bottom. I've never felt so alone and scared as I did at that moment. But you were there, and I realized I wasn't alone. That I didn't have to be." Her eyes met his. "And that I don't *want* to be."

Her words slammed into him like a hurricane, causing his breath to catch in his chest. The right response escaped him at that moment, and all he could manage was "Come here."

She crossed the short distance and threw herself against him. Brenna buried her face against his chest and breathed deeply while her arms gripped him like a life rope. He could feel the tension leaving her in increments, each slow breath seeming to ease her. Occasionally her breath stuttered suspiciously, like a sob, but the trembles that moved over her slowly dissipated.

He didn't know how long they stood there, the warmth of Brenna seeping into his bones as he breathed in the sunshine citrus scent of her hair and stroked the soft strands. The iron grip of her hands finally loosened, and then began to smooth a gentle path up and down his sides and over his chest. When she lifted her head and met his eyes again, he could see a bit of his Brenna emerging from behind the fatigue and worry.

Rising up on her tiptoes, Brenna wrapped a hand

around his neck and pulled his mouth to hers. The fire, the passion, the raw desire—it was all there, and it moved though him like an electrical current. But it was tempered by something else in her kiss.

That feeling shook him, and he groaned as he lifted her off her feet, loving the way she clung to him, moving them both the short distance down the hall to his bed, where he pulled her down on top of him.

Brenna deepened the kiss, threading her fingers through his hair, scratching her nails gently against his scalp. She sighed his name against his neck as his arms tightened around her and molded her body to his, and he felt another tremor—of pleasure this time—shake her gently.

Brenna didn't want to be alone. Didn't have to be alone.

Neither did he.

The headache throbbing behind her eyes was growing steadily worse. She should have gone back to bed after the first phone call of the morning. The nice woman in North Napa who'd heard Brenna was selling off her grapes and wanted to buy a couple of bins' worth to make jam had been a blow to her ego. Her mother's Pinot Noir grapes, being made into *jam*. Ugh. At the time she'd thought with a starting note like that the day could only get better.

Then Ted had brought her more bad news. Her head was still spinning from *that* information, but she was holding it together. Tears would not help the situation any.

Now she was up to her ears in numbers—including the ones Jack had crunched yesterday—and the bottom line was just plain depressing. As the weight settled more firmly on her shoulders, she seriously re-thought her earlier resolution not to cry. A good let-it-all-out bawl might make her feel a little better, at least.

No. She took a deep cleansing breath and let it out slowly. As Jack had said last night, she would get through this. If she just kept repeating that to herself, she might actually begin to believe it.

Jack wasn't an early riser, and he'd been sleeping soundly when she crawled out of bed at dawn. Now she heard rattling in the kitchen, the unmistakable sounds of someone after a cup of coffee. When Jack entered the office a few minutes later he held two cups, one of which he placed in front of her as he bent to kiss the top of her head. "Did you get any sleep?"

"Only a little," she confessed. "It's hard to turn my brain off."

"What's that?" Jack asked, reading the notepad in front of her.

She didn't need to look at it again. "Only the latest bad news."

"And?"

"Ted's worried about soil contamination—from the runoff from the fire. All the chemicals and the ashes in the water have drained into the vines. There's no telling what it will do. We're going to lose the acre behind the winery. Maybe a little more than that."

Jack's mouth twisted a little. "Sorry to hear that. How long will it take to replace them?"

"After we replace the soil and replant it will still be three to five years before we can get any fruit off the new vines."

"Ouch. At least I know your insurance policy *does* cover that loss."

She could tell Jack was trying to be upbeat for her sake, but, while she appreciated the gesture, he seemed to be missing the point entirely. "The money's not the issue," she explained.

He glanced at the sheet of figures in front of her. "That kind of money should be."

He just didn't get it. "Jack, my great-grandfather planted those vines, almost sixty years ago. They're healthy, productive vines—the fruit is amazing—and I'm going to have to rip them out of the ground. Trust me, the money isn't the problem."

"But they *can* be replaced."

Hadn't he been listening? "No, they can't."

"Only you could have a sentimental attachment to a plant." There was a small chuckle in his voice that sent her hackles up.

She spun in her chair to face him squarely. "What's that supposed to mean?"

"Don't get your back up, Bren. I'm just saying that you're emotionally invested in this place—"

"Well, *yeah*," she interrupted. But he knew that. He knew how she felt about Amante Verano.

He continued as if she hadn't said anything. "To the

extent that you don't always see the big picture. They're just vines. We'll replace them with something better."

His words cut her, and the hurt ran deep. "They're slightly more than 'just vines' to me. They can't be replaced that easily—much less with something 'better.' Those vines are the backbone and history of Amante Verano. I'm sorry if that offends your MBA, but that's the truth." She could hear the snap in her voice, and she tried unsuccessfully to tone it down.

"'Backbone and history'? Bren, you have to keep your emotions separate from your business."

He didn't know her at all. "That's your answer for everything. 'Keep your business and your personal life apart.' Sorry, but it's not so clear-cut for me. This is my *home* as well as my livelihood. I can't really separate the two."

"Then it's a good thing I'm here, isn't it?"

Not necessarily. His grin wasn't working on her this time. "Are you implying…?"

"I'm not implying anything. You said it yourself— you're too close to be objective."

She could quite happily strangle him at that moment. "Wine-making is a very *sub*jective business. I don't have to be completely objective."

"Then it's a good thing I still own half of this place, isn't it?"

Anger erupted in her chest. The nerve… *That* was the last straw. Almost blinded by the red haze in front of her eyes, she jerked open desk drawers until she found the manila folder she was looking for. Inside it was the sale agreement. Grabbing a pen off the desk, she flipped to the last page and scrawled her signature at the bottom.

In two steps she was around the desk. She slapped the agreement against his chest, where he grabbed it reflexively. "There. Now you don't own any of it."

"Bren…"

"Amante Verano may be a mess, but it's my mess. And I won't have you patronizing me or telling me the proper way to run *my* business. I'll get through this, remember?"

"I'm trying to help you here, Bren."

"I don't want or need your help. Now, get the hell off my property."

Not waiting for Jack's response, she let her ire carry her back to Max's desk—*her* desk—where she turned her back on him and stared blindly at the numbers on the paper in front of her.

She heard his sigh, but his words were clipped, angry. "If that's the way you want it, Bren, *fine*. Good luck."

On that note, Jack left the room. A minute later she heard the back door close and Jack's car start up. She sat quietly until the noise faded into the distance, then sagged back against the chair. Closing her eyes, she felt the finality of what had just happened wash over her.

Once again she'd lost Jack. Driven him away. The pain that sliced through her put anything she'd felt in the last two days to shame. The bands tightening around her chest made it hard to breathe, and her heart sat like a stone in her chest.

She could feel the tears burning her eyes; she could

feel the sobs trapped in her throat just waiting to be set free. *Tears won't help*, she reminded herself.

But it was too late. She laid her head on her desk and cried.

CHAPTER TWELVE

IN THE two weeks since Brenna had thrown him off her property he'd had no word from her or Amante Verano. Not that he'd expected it; her intent had been very clear, and, if he'd had any doubts, the arrival by courier of the anklet he'd given her a few days later would have clarified it. He and Brenna were back where they'd started a few weeks ago. *Ex.*

That bothered him. A lot more than he'd thought it would.

His life had quickly settled right back into its normal routine, and he was bored stiff by it. He missed the energy and spark Brenna brought just by being in the same room. Everything moved along like before, but it felt monotonous and bland. Plus, he was getting damned tired of everyone agreeing with him all the time.

Business was good. The New York deal had gone through without a hitch, and Garrett Properties was now established on both coasts. Profits were up. His employees and his stockholders were equally happy with him. He'd received notice just yesterday he'd be receiving an award for "Outstanding Philanthropic Efforts" in the city of San Francisco.

He was having a hard time dredging up enthusiasm for any of it, and he could trace his general dissatisfaction with life straight back to Brenna.

Even though Brenna was ignoring him, that didn't mean he didn't have access to what was going on at Amante Verano. His company still had a twenty-five percent interest in the vineyard, so he was fully up-to-date with Brenna's recovery efforts.

They weren't going well. Amante Verano just didn't have the funds on hand to tide them over until settlements could be reached with the insurance companies and the building could be replaced. Now the bank had turned down her request to have her line of credit increased. He fully understood why: the vineyard was a very bad risk at the moment.

Brenna was hemorrhaging money as she tried to get her feet back under her, but it would be a full year before she'd even get another crop in, even longer before she'd have wine ready to sell.

She was teetering on the edge of bankruptcy already. The loss on Jack's books would be negligible. He could tell, though, by the update he'd received from his people, that Brenna knew she was on the precipice.

It had to be killing her, but he knew Brenna would never come to him for help now. Her stubborn pride wouldn't let her—not after the way they'd left things. She'd accused him of not fully understanding her, but he did. Probably better than anyone else. While he might not understand her emotional attachment to

Amante Verano, he did understand it was as much a part
of her as her red hair and her temper.

And he loved her in spite of it.

He sighed and swiveled his chair around, taking in
the view of the Golden Gate Bridge, where buses full
of tourists were making their way out to wine country.
A month ago some of them would have been headed to
Brenna's, but now there wasn't much there to interest
the tourists. The great irony was that now there was
something at Amante Verano of great interest to *him*.

He was in love with his ex-wife… Lord, could his
life be any more screwed up?

But he still didn't know exactly how he could help
her right things at the winery. He had plenty of the one
thing Brenna needed most right now—money—but the
chances of her accepting it if he offered…? Slim.

He hadn't wanted anything to do with owning a
winery, or investing in one, and he'd succeeded. He'd
wanted out, and Brenna had thrown him out.

Be careful what you wish for.

But all routes weren't closed to him. As Brenna had
said, the Garrett name alone could open many doors. She
might not want his help, but she was going to get it.

It was the least he could do for her.

As he picked up the phone, he knew somewhere
Max was laughing his head off.

The idleness was driving Brenna crazy. She'd never had
so much free time on her hands. Every morning when
she woke up and realized she didn't have a ton of work
waiting for her in the winery, the blow was just as fresh.

And spending the day fielding frustrating phone calls and watching her bottom line sink deeper and deeper into the red wasn't any better than having nothing to do at all.

But the disaster of her professional life had only highlighted something else: how little personal life she actually had. No hobbies. Few friends beyond Di and Ted, and those she did have buried under their own post-crush work in *their* wineries. Somehow, that used to seem like enough, but now it didn't. Playing Solitaire on her laptop was a poor excuse for a life.

Jack was right: she needed to get off the property more.

Jack. The thought of him brought a chest-crushing wave of pain that hadn't subsided any over the last couple of weeks. Without the busy work Amante Verano used to provide she had ample time to think about Jack, and everything that had transpired, until the pain and emptiness overwhelmed her.

She'd let her temper get the best of her. Even if she tried to blame her last outburst on a really bad day, she had to admit that it had been more than just stress egging her on. The amount of time she'd had to think had given her clarity on a couple of topics. She had used the vineyard as a safety blanket all these years: no need to mourn the loss of Jack when she had Amante Verano to immerse herself in. It had still been a connection to Jack—however tenuous—but now that was gone.

Losing Jack a second time had sucked all the blood out of her heart, and she felt like a zombie wandering though what was left of her life. Facing the destruction of the winery had been much easier when Jack was here; now it seemed insurmountable.

Late at night, when there was even less to occupy her, Jack's absence was harder to bear. Jack had been a safe harbor when she'd hit bottom, and she missed that feeling of strength he gave her by just being there.

Oh, who was she trying to fool? She just missed *him*. The pain she'd felt when she'd signed the divorce papers was nothing compared to this—because this time she'd gone in eyes open, without all those teenage romanticized ideas.

And she'd fallen even harder than before.

She'd quit crying herself to sleep simply because she'd run out of tears.

Brenna blew her hair out of her face and stared blankly at her computer screen, trying to remember what she was supposed to be doing. Good Lord, she couldn't even concentrate on the disaster in front of her because of Jack.

From her seat on the couch she saw Di through the French doors, shortcutting her way into the house through the vines. Dianne was moving faster than normal, and she practically burst through the doors. "'Every day is a great day at Amante Verano', right?"

"I wouldn't say *great*, Di," Brenna answered, but the excited grin on Dianne's face was enough to toss a shot of hope into the bleakness.

"Well, this should definitely make this day a little better for you." Dianne waved a letter at her.

"Because…?" she prompted.

"The bank has approved your application to extend our line of credit."

"What? They shot us down as too big a risk."

"Obviously they've reconsidered. Look, Brenna." Di handed her the letter. "Money. Look at all those zeros. Enough to tide us over until the insurance pays out and we get back on our feet." Di was almost dancing with excitement.

It didn't make any sense, but there, in black and white, was the lifeline she needed. It seemed too good to be true. "Hand me the phone, will you?"

Dianne did as she asked, but as she handed it over added, "Who are you calling?"

"Mia Ryan at the bank. I want to be sure this isn't a computer glitch before I start spending money I don't really have."

Dianne raised an eyebrow, then shrugged as Brenna dialed.

"Mia, it's Brenna Walsh. Can you tell me what's up with our line of credit?"

"Of course, Brenna." She could hear Mia's fingers on her keyboard. "How are things?"

"If the letter I got today is for real, then things are about to be much better."

"I'm glad to hear it. Here we go. Let me see…" There was a long pause as Mia consulted something, then Brenna heard the keyboard again. "Interesting…"

"Interesting? How?"

"Your LOC request was reopened two days ago and approved based on an increase in your cash on hand and a guarantee on the debt."

"Cash on hand?" She didn't *have* any cash on hand.

Money was flowing out of Amante Verano like a river, not in. "Are you sure?"

"That's what it says." Mia read Brenna her account balance, and Brenna's good mood evaporated.

"That's a mistake."

"I don't think so, Brenna. Let me check something."

Brenna tried to be patient as Mia put her on hold, but Dianne's questions in the interim were only increasing her confusion and agitation about the situation. She held up a hand to silence her as Mia came back on the line.

"Okay, Brenna. I found it, and it's all correct. Jack Garrett deposited the money into your account at the same time he guaranteed the LOC."

"Jack?" Her throat seemed to be closing and words were hard to get out. "Surely you mean Garrett Properties. They're the other partner. Not Jack."

"No." Mia sounded as if she thought Brenna was a marble or two shy of a game. "It was Jack Garrett personally. I can see the scan of the check and the LOC agreement. Are you okay, Brenna?" she added, as Brenna started to choke.

Di's eyes widened and she handed Brenna her glass of water.

Brenna waved her away. "I'm fine," she said, to Di and Mia both. "Thanks for checking, Mia."

"Anytime. And good luck."

Brenna hung up the phone and met Dianne's amazed stare. Her world had just turned slightly sideways. The hope of financial rescue was tempered by the surety there was a mistake, a catch somehow. But that funny feeling in her stomach at the thought of Jack...

"Did I hear that right?" Di asked. "*Jack* had something to do with this?"

"Mia says he personally guaranteed our line of credit *and* deposited a nice chunk of cash into our account." The words sounded too unreal to believe, even to her, and yet she had confirmation from the bank.

From the look on Dianne's face, Brenna knew Di was finding it hard to believe, too. "And you didn't know? He didn't tell you?"

"Do I look like I knew Jack was going to do this?"

Di shrugged. "So what does this mean?"

"I don't know. I find it hard to believe Jack's had a sudden desire to invest in a winery. Much less one that's teetering on the edge of disaster."

"Me, too. He was so adamant about…"

"Yeah, I know." *But he was starting to come around—at least until I kicked him off the property.*

"Then this is about you." Di's smile turned smug.

"Me?" she squeaked as her heart did a flip-flop in her chest. "No, it must have something to do with protecting Garrett Properties' share. Or something…" Brenna pushed herself off the couch and headed down the hall. "I'll see you later, Di."

"Where are you going?"

Where else? "San Francisco. To talk to Jack."

While she had the nerve.

Golf tournaments. He'd sponsor them, but he wasn't going to play in them. He responded to Libby Winston's email invite with a vague claim of other plans. Garrett Properties would send a check, and that would have to do. Libby's not-so-subtle request that he accompany her was better left ignored.

The intercom on his desk beeped. "Mr. Garrett, there's a Brenna Walsh here to see you. She doesn't have an appointment—"

His pulse kicked up. He didn't wait to hear the rest. "Send her in." *Brenna, here?* He stood and rounded his desk as his office door opened and Brenna walked in.

"Hi, Jack." She looked much better than she had two weeks ago—a little more color to her cheeks, no shadows under her eyes—but her face was still pinched with stress. "Sorry to barge in."

He hadn't expected to be so happy to see her. Or that he wouldn't know what to say to her. Casual small talk seemed ridiculous, considering everything. "It's not a problem, Bren. How are things at Amante Verano?"

She raised an eyebrow. "You mean you don't know?"

So she knew already. The bank must have moved quickly. But her voice lacked any heat behind the sarcasm, so it was hard for him to tell how she was choosing to take the news—that raised eyebrow wasn't offering much help.

"Touché. Yes, I know how things are businesswise at Amante Verano. How are you and Dianne and Ted doing?"

A shrug. "We're getting by. It's a struggle, but we're doing what we can."

God, he was tempted to reach for her, but…

"Look, I'll cut to the chase." Brenna moved to the

chair in front of his desk and sat. "I want to know why you are the guarantor on my line of credit."

Business it was, then. He went back to his chair and faced her across the expanse of his desk. "Because the bank wouldn't extend it without one. Not even for me. You're too high a risk at the moment."

"You can say that again," she muttered. "And the money that's appeared in my account?"

It was his turn to shrug. "Consider it a gift."

Brenna's mouth fell open. "That kind of money is not a gift. There's no way I can accept it. Surely you know that? I don't need your charity."

Obviously she'd forgotten he knew the state of her finances at the moment. "Then consider it a loan. You can pay it back when you get back on your feet."

That seemed to surprise her. "Just like that? You don't even want me to sign an IOU?"

"I don't think we need one. Do you?"

Brenna eyed him carefully. "Are you drunk?"

"No."

"Did you take up drugs? Hit your head against something hard?"

He was hard-pressed not to laugh. "No and no."

"Then you've gone insane."

Bren did have that effect on him. "Possibly. Why?"

"Because sane people don't go sticking money into their ex-wives' accounts or guaranteeing their loans."

"Maybe I believe Amante Verano is a good investment."

He saw the way her spine straightened with pride before she caught herself. "You really have lost your mind. You don't want to be in this business. You didn't want to own part of a winery when times were good, so why would you want to invest in one now? Considering the shape we're in…"

"I just want you to be happy, Bren, and I know getting Amante Verano back on track will make you happy."

He could see the suspicion in her eyes. "I don't get it. What's in it for you, Jack?"

This was it. Time to put up or shut up. He let the question hang there for a moment, until Brenna started shifting uncomfortably in her seat, her impatience starting to fuel her temper.

"Well, Jack? Tell me what's in it for you."

"You."

The word seemed to hang in the air between them, bringing their conversation—if that was what it could be called—to a screeching halt. All the breath seemed to rush out of her lungs, and she couldn't quite make her body remember to inhale again.

"I don't— I mean—I don't quite understand. What do you mean me?" *What happened to keeping business and personal lives separate?*

Jack met her eyes levelly. "You wouldn't be you without Amante Verano. I'm not saying I fully understand the connection—but then I don't understand the attraction to golf either. But I *do* understand that it's important to you and that it makes you happy." He sighed. "If I have to pump money into your winery to make you happy again and make you *you*, I will."

That was a lot to process all at once. "You'd do that? For me?"

Exasperated, Jack rolled his eyes. "Yes, you infuriating woman."

The disconnect was too much. "But you don't *want* a winery."

There was that even stare again. "But I want you."

Her heart jumped in her chest as his words brought tears to the corners of her eyes. "Really?"

"Bren…"

She stood, stalling for a moment while she tried to make sense of everything. "I thought you just felt sorry for me. Or that you were trying to protect your company's bottom line. I couldn't believe you'd…not after the way I treated you."

Jack came around the desk and leaned against it. "You've got a temper, Bren. I know that. But you should know by now that I do, too." He caught her arm and pulled her around to look at him. "I'm telling you that I understand how much your vineyard means to you, and I shouldn't have discounted that."

"But that's the thing, Jack. I've had plenty of time to think over the last few weeks." Now that she knew what she wanted to say, she couldn't get the words out fast enough. "Yeah, it's bad at the vineyard right now, but that's only been a part of the general suckiness of my life. I realized I've used Amante Verano as an excuse for far too long. I used it as a safety net after the divorce, and it's become a habit. But what I've been going through with the vineyard is nothing compared to what I've gone through not having you."

It was his turn to look surprised, but the look quickly gentled into something beautiful. It gave her the courage to say the rest.

"I told you that night after the fire that I realized I didn't want to be alone. But it's more than just not being alone. I want to be with *you*."

His eyes began to glow with warmth—and desire. It sent a shiver through her. "Really, Bren."

"Yeah. And I want more than that."

He nodded as he crossed his arms over his chest. "Ah, back to more…"

Now was not the time to back down. "Yes. It's going to take more than just throwing money at my business to make me happy. And you did say you wanted to make me happy."

"I'll bite, Bren. What more do you want?"

"You."

The brilliant smile that crossed his face made the last few weeks of hell all worthwhile. This time, when Jack reached for her, there was no hesitation at all as she walked into his arms. As he pulled her against him she felt the warmth of his body seep into hers, thawing the chill that had gripped her since he'd left. Finally her heart seemed to be beating at a normal rhythm again. *This* was right. She'd been crazy to fight it.

Then he kissed her, and her heartbeat was no longer normal at all.

"I love you, Jack. I always have."

Jack pressed his forehead to hers. "And I love you. Let's go home."

Home. The thought thrilled her and twinged her

heart at the same time. It must have shown on her face, because Jack pulled back and his brows knitted together in concern.

"What's wrong, Bren?"

She was not going to let anything ruin this moment. "Nothing." She raised up on her tiptoes to kiss him again, but Jack held her at arm's length.

"You might as well tell me now. Our brilliant lack of communication skills is what got us divorced last time. I don't want to go there again."

Again? Was Jack already thinking…? She paused that happy thought. He was right. "It's hard for me to consider a hotel home. No matter how nice it is," she qualified.

Jack nodded. "But Amante Verano isn't home for me, you know?"

She had no illusions. "I know. I'll just—"

"How do you feel about Bel Marin Keys?"

"Excuse me?"

He cocked his head. "Or Novato, maybe? That's not too crowded. You don't have to live directly on the property, do you?"

His meaning finally registered. "You'd leave San Francisco?"

Jack slid his hands up and down her arms. "We'll compromise, Bren. Find someplace between here and there to live."

"I can't believe you'd leave the city?"

"If I have to, to keep you happy, yes."

"You make me happy, Jack." She paused. "Even if you do annoy me sometimes."

He laughed. "You can annoy me whenever you want. I've felt half-dead without you around."

"Me, too." She tugged on his hand. "So let's go."

Jack resisted the tug. "One last thing. About the money I put in your account. I think we should come up with some kind of arrangement."

Business and personal life separate. *Right.* "I understand. How about—?"

He held up a hand to stop her. "Remember my first offer? The one I made that night by the hot tub?"

Ugh. "It's not my favorite memory, but, yes."

"I want to amend that offer. You can have Amante Verano—and whatever you need to get it back on its feet—but it will cost you more than just one night. Possibly a lifetime."

She should smack him, but instead she mirrored his cheeky grin. "Where do I sign?"

EPILOGUE

BRENNA winced as Jack's construction crew knocked down the wall of what used to be her kitchen. "Max would not be happy about this."

Jack put his arm around her shoulder and squeezed. "Max would be thrilled. Trust me on that. His two favorite things—hotels and wine—in one convenient location."

Jack was right, but it was still difficult to see her home gutted and rearranged. What *used* to be her home, she amended. She didn't live here anymore, hadn't lived here in almost two years. It was wrong to let the building continue to sit empty, but it still hurt to see that gaping hole.

He placed a finger under her chin and lifted her face to his. "You do know the building can't feel anything, right?"

She elbowed him in return, then pulled the collar of her jacket up around her neck as the March wind picked up. She looked around the patio, which looked as bad as the rest of the place. Power tools, saw-horses, bags of concrete and all the other debris of destruction and construction littered what had used to be her quiet, serene escape. At least the plants were still alive, but they looked odd, sitting around the drained hot tub and swimming pool. "It just feels weird."

"It's going to be very profitable, though. Dianne is already getting calls—she's booking out rooms and we're still six weeks from the Grand Opening."

"I know. She's giddy about it. I never dreamed she'd take the idea and run with it like this." Dianne had embraced Jack's idea to open up Amante Verano for wine seminars, using what had used to be Brenna's house as a bed-and-breakfast for people who wanted to learn more about the process of making wine than the usual hour-long tour provided. Before she knew it, her simple little vineyard had suddenly exploded into a full-on tourist destination.

And now that word was out that Garrett Properties was opening a boutique hotel on the vineyard property, everyone from wine aficionados to brides looking for a unique wedding venue was knocking down her doors.

Metaphorically, at least. The house currently didn't *have* any doors—unless she counted the ones leaning against the side of the building, waiting to be installed.

Brenna had taken to hiding in her lab or her office most of the time she was on the property these days, but she'd made the mistake of surfacing just in time to see this blow dealt to the house. The place looked like…
"Will it actually be finished in six weeks?"

"It'll be finished in five." Jack winked at her. "By the way, that wine magazine you like so much is sending someone out to cover the Grand Opening reception."

"Interesting. Two years ago they wouldn't give me the time of day. They weren't interested in Brenna Walsh. Brenna Garrett is a different story, it seems."

"See? there are all kinds of perks to being a Garrett."

"Many," she agreed, rising up on her tiptoes to kiss him. Stepping back, she shaded her eyes from the sun and looked up at him. "What are you doing here today anyway? I thought you were going to Sacramento for a meeting."

Jack shrugged. "I didn't feel like it. I sent Martin instead."

"Tsk, tsk," she scolded. "Blowing off work like that…"

He was unrepentant. "It's just another one of the perks of being a Garrett. Anyway, I needed to come check on the progress here." He looked around and shrugged. "Seems to be moving along fine. I guess I'm done for the day."

Jack slid his fingers through hers and pulled her close again. "What say we go home early?"

She mentally ran down her to-do list. "Are you insane? Some of us don't have half a dozen minions on hand to run our businesses for us."

"Then hire some."

"You run your business and I'll run mine. You're a silent partner, remember?"

"Silent, but not mute."

"Mute would be delightful," Brenna grumbled.

"Ah, but then I couldn't tell you what I have planned

for this afternoon…" Pulling her close, he whispered ideas that had her toes curling and her heart pounding in anticipation.

"You are evil, Jack Garrett. It was your idea to start all this expansion and construction, and *now* you want me to play hooky?"

"I just want you, period." He shrugged. "Seriously, Bren, this place is getting too big for you to do everything. Even Dianne has a fleet of assistants now. You can't keep doing everything on your own. You're wearing yourself out. You're so tired lately."

It was the opening she needed. The one she'd been waiting for the last few days. Now seemed to be the right time. "You're right. I should hire some people. Including an assistant vintner or two."

Jack eyebrows flew up in surprise. "It's about damn time. I never thought I'd hear you say that."

She needed to sit for this conversation, but all her patio furniture was either stacked in the yard or being used to hold construction paraphernalia. She walked to the edge of the hot tub and sat, dangling her feet into the emptiness. "Yeah, well, I'm going to need the help soon enough. This year's crush is going to be a bit difficult for me."

Jack joined her, studying her face curiously. "Because…?" he prompted.

"Did Max ever give you the lecture on the three things he wanted most?"

Jack shook his head and looked at her questioningly.

"Number one was a five-star hotel in Manhattan."

He smiled smugly. "Done."

"Number two was a gold-medal wine."

"Done—thanks to you." He reached for her hand again and squeezed her fingers.

She nodded at the compliment, then took a deep breath. "Number three was a grandchild."

A small smile began to form on his face. "And...?"

"Well, he's going to get one of those, too."

Jack pulled her close, one hand against her back, the other splayed over her still-flat stomach. The small smile had grown into an all-out grin, and it told her how happy he was with her news. "See? I told you Max didn't like to be thwarted."

Huh? "When did you tell me that?"

"Right after Max died. We were out here, remember? In the hot tub."

It took a second, but the memory came. She snorted. "How could I forget that night? Among *other things* we won't mention—" she narrowed her eyes at him "—you called me a wine snob."

Jack laughed. "And you called me a jerk."

"I wasn't wrong," she countered.

"Neither was I—about that part, at least."

She feigned shock. "You're admitting you were wrong about something? That's a first."

Jack made a face at her. "You asked me what made me happy."

She'd almost forgotten. "Oh, yeah. You said something about cars and Scotch, or something ridiculous."

He nudged her arm with his elbow playfully. "Ask me again."

She'd bite. The twinkle in his eye was irresistible. "What makes you happy, Jack?"

He kissed her, sending a thrill through her, then smiled as he cupped her face.

"You."

Coming Next Month

from **Harlequin Presents®**. Available October 26, 2010.

#2951 THE PREGNANCY SHOCK
Lynne Graham
The Drakos Baby

#2952 SOPHIE AND THE SCORCHING SICILIAN
Kim Lawrence
The Balfour Brides

#2953 FALCO: THE DARK GUARDIAN
Sandra Marton
The Orsini Brothers

#2954 CHOSEN BY THE SHEIKH
Kim Lawrence and Lynn Raye Harris

#2955 THE SABBIDES SECRET BABY
Jacqueline Baird

#2956 CASTELLANO'S MISTRESS OF REVENGE
Melanie Milburne

Coming Next Month

from **Harlequin Presents® EXTRA**. Available November 9, 2010.

#125 SHAMEFUL SECRET, SHOTGUN WEDDING
Sharon Kendrick
Snowkissed and Seduced

#126 THE TWELVE NIGHTS OF CHRISTMAS
Sarah Morgan
Snowkissed and Seduced

#127 EVERY GIRL'S SECRET FANTASY
Robyn Grady
Rogues & Rebels

#128 UNTAMEABLE ROGUE
Kelly Hunter
Rogues & Rebels

LARGER-PRINT BOOKS!

HARLEQUIN *Presents*~

PASSION GUARANTEED SEDUCTION

GET 2 FREE LARGER-PRINT NOVELS PLUS 2 FREE GIFTS!

YES! Please send me 2 FREE LARGER-PRINT Harlequin Presents® novels and my 2 FREE gifts (gifts are worth about $10). After receiving them, if I don't wish to receive any more books, I can return the shipping statement marked "cancel". If I don't cancel, I will receive 6 brand-new novels every month and be billed just $4.55 per book in the U.S. or $5.24 per book in Canada. That's a saving of at least 13% off the cover price! It's quite a bargain! Shipping and handling is just 50¢ per book.* I understand that accepting the 2 free books and gifts places me under no obligation to buy anything. I can always return a shipment and cancel at any time. Even if I never buy another book, the two free books and gifts are mine to keep forever.

176/376 HDN E5NG

Name	(PLEASE PRINT)	
Address		Apt. #
City	State/Prov.	Zip/Postal Code

Signature (if under 18, a parent or guardian must sign)

Mail to the **Harlequin Reader Service:**
IN U.S.A.: P.O. Box 1867, Buffalo, NY 14240-1867
IN CANADA: P.O. Box 609, Fort Erie, Ontario L2A 5X3

Not valid for current subscribers to Harlequin Presents Larger-Print books.

Are you a subscriber to Harlequin Presents books and want to receive the larger-print edition? Call 1-800-873-8635 today!

* Terms and prices subject to change without notice. Prices do not include applicable taxes. Sales tax applicable in N.Y. Canadian residents will be charged applicable provincial taxes and GST. Offer not valid in Quebec. This offer is limited to one order per household. All orders subject to approval. Credit or debit balances in a customer's account(s) may be offset by any other outstanding balance owed by or to the customer. Please allow 4 to 6 weeks for delivery. Offer available while quantities last.

HPLP10R

HARLEQUIN®

A Romance
FOR EVERY MOOD™

Spotlight on
Inspirational

Wholesome romances
that touch the heart and soul.

See the next page
to enjoy a sneak peek from
the Love Inspired® Suspense
inspirational series.

*See below for a sneak peek from
our inspirational line, Love Inspired® Suspense*

*Enjoy this heart-stopping excerpt from
RUNNING BLIND
by top author Shirlee McCoy,
available November 2010!*

*The mission trip to Mexico was supposed to be an
adventure. But the thrill turns sour when Jenna Dougherty
and her roommate Magdalena are kidnapped.*

"It's okay. I'm here to help." The voice was as deep as the darkness, but Jenna Dougherty didn't believe the lie. She could do nothing but lie still as hands slid down her arms, felt the rope around her wrists.

"I'm going to use a knife to cut you free, Jenna. Hold still."

The cold blade of a knife pressed close to her head before her gag fell away.

"I—" she started, but her mouth was dry, and she could do nothing but suck in air.

"Shhh. Whatever needs to be said can be said when we're out of here." Nick spoke quietly, his hand gentle on her cheek. There and gone as he sliced through the ropes on her wrists and ankles.

He pulled her upright. "Come on. We may be on borrowed time."

"I can't leave my friend," Jenna rasped out.

"There's no one here. Just us."

"She has to be here." Jenna took a step away.

"There's no one here. Let's go before that changes."

"It's dark. Maybe if we find a light…"

"What did you say?"

"We need to turn on the light. I can't leave until I know that—"

"What can you see, Jenna?"

"Nothing."

"No shadows? No light?"

"No."

"It's broad daylight. There's light spilling in from the window I climbed in through. You can't see it?"

She went cold at his words.

"I can't see anything."

"You've got a nasty bruise on your forehead. Maybe that has something to do with it." His fingers traced the tender flesh on her forehead.

"It doesn't matter *how* it happened. I'm blind!"

Can Nick help Jenna find her friend or will chasing this trail have Jenna running blindly again into danger?

Find out in RUNNING BLIND, available in November 2010 only from Love Inspired Suspense.

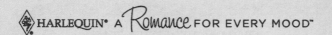